Praise for Zoran

"Winner of the 2003 World Fantasy Award . . . Zoran Živković is an immensely talented fabulist whose work is somewhat reminiscent of Italo Calvino's wry and delightfully surreal postmodern fictions."

—Paul Witcover, *Realms of Fantasy*

Other Books by Zoran Živković

HIDDEN CAMERA

Zoran Živković

Translation by Alice Copple-Tošić

Dalkey Archive Press
Normal · London

Originally published in Serbian as *Skrivena Kamera* by Polaris, 2003
Copyright © 2003 by Zoran Živković
English translation copyright © 2005 by Alice Copple-Tošić

First U.S. edition, 2005

Library of Congress Cataloging-in-Publication Data:

Živković, Zoran.
    [Skrivena kamera. English]
    Hidden camera / Zoran Živković ; translated by Alice Copple-Tošić.—
1st ed.
        p. cm.
    ISBN 1-56478-412-6 (pbk. : alk. paper)
    I. Tošić, Alice. II. Title.

PG1419.36.I954S5713 2005
891.8'236—dc22
                                                        2005049210

Partially funded by a grant from the Illinois Arts Council, a state agency.

Dalkey Archive Press is a nonprofit organization located at
Milner Library (Illinois State University) and distributed in the UK
by Turnaround Publisher Services Ltd. (London).

www.dalkeyarchive.com

Printed on permanent/durable acid-free paper and bound in the
United States of America.

HIDDEN CAMERA

1

I found the envelope wedged in my apartment door.

That was unusual. The mailman had never delivered a letter that way before. Why hadn't he dropped it into the mailbox with the others? I'd just collected the mail he'd left, as I always do when I come back from work. While the elevator took me up to the third floor, I gave the mail a quick look. Nothing special: a bill and three advertisements. I put my briefcase on the floor, stuck the letters from the mailbox under my arm, took the envelope and inspected it on both sides. That settled one question but raised another. The mailman had nothing to do with this letter. He delivers mail without information about the sender, but not without information about the receiver. Among other reasons, because he wouldn't know to whom to deliver it. No writing defaced the whiteness of the long envelope. But who had wedged it into the door frame if not the mailman?

As I unlocked the door, it occurred to me what this might be. It was another advertisement, except they hadn't sent it the usual way, through the mail, but distributed it door to door, and in addition wrapped it in a veil of mysterious anonymity. They probably figured it would get more attention that way. I, for example, had already given it more attention than the three advertisements from my mailbox got; they would end up in the garbage without being opened. Who knows, I might even open the letter. It was very light, as though there

3

was nothing inside. Someone had put considerable effort into arousing the curiosity of potential customers.

The only thing I couldn't figure out was how the deliverer had entered the building. The entrance is always locked and it's highly unlikely that any of the tenants would let a stranger inside if he called on the intercom and said he wanted to wedge advertisements in everyone's door. He must have tricked someone. Those people are cunning. How else could they succeed at their work? Before I entered my apartment I looked at the front door of the other apartment on my landing. There was no white envelope there. They must have taken it inside already.

I hung my coat and hat on the coat rack in the vestibule and went into the living room. I dropped my briefcase on a chair, put the letter on the coffee table and rushed to the aquarium. My tropical fish are more important than anything else. I have to feed them at 5:30 sharp. First I checked the thermostat to make sure the water was the right temperature, and then the air pump with its jet of bubbles streaming towards the surface. Then I took the plastic top off the can and started sprinkling mealy fish food onto the water. The fish immediately began a voracious hunt after the little lumps, fighting unnecessarily over some pieces while other bits of food slowly sank to the bottom.

I'm not fond of animals and would never have a dog, cat or parakeet in my apartment, let alone any other species. It's not because I don't want their company—many people who live alone like I do solve the problem of loneliness this way, whether they admit it or not—but

4

because I'd then be confronted with responsibilities that I couldn't properly fulfill. Unlike larger animals, fish don't require much care. It's enough to feed them twice a day at a specific time. The tank's simple equipment made sure the proper conditions were maintained in the aquarium.

Once, however, the heater broke. During the night, water had somehow come in contact with the electric wires. In the morning I found the whole little school of fish floating lifelessly on the surface. I wasn't too upset. That same day I bought a new heater and new fish—and everything was the same as before. Someone might conclude from this that I have no feelings, but this isn't true. The death of the little tropical creatures would have been harder on me had I been on more intimate terms with them. But there had been nothing more than reciprocated indifference. The fish were only aware of my existence during the brief moments when I fed them, and then only as some impersonal force that acted kindly towards them for some unknown reason. In all other circumstances they didn't pay me the slightest attention.

I paid quite a bit of attention to them, however, although not as recognizable individuals with any feelings of attachment. This is actually why I had bought them, spurred on by an article in the newspaper that suggested different ways to relax. I would turn off all the lights in the living room except for the one above the aquarium, put on a CD, settle into the armchair nearby, and let myself unwind as I watched them. Sometimes this lasted quite a while. It was never less than half an hour, and once I stayed there next to the fish for two hours and twenty-four minutes, only getting up to change the CD. The length of this aquarium therapy depended on how stressed I was. But even the greatest stress would finally start to ease before the soundless, chaotic movement of colorful shapes that I stared at as though hypnotized.

During one of the first sessions something curious crossed my mind. I thought about how the fish and I lived in two parallel worlds that had almost nothing to do with each other, and yet were of mutual benefit. What the fish received from my world was quite elementary: food and warmth. I, in return, received from theirs something immeasurably more complicated: inner tranquility. If I wanted to thank them for this gift, how could I possibly do it? How could I explain the concept of inner tranquility to beings without a soul? I couldn't. Some things can pass through the membrane that divides parallel worlds and some things can't.

The fish were now taken care of until morning. As soon as I had had something to eat myself, I would be in need of their services. I'd just been through another depressing day. Only the ignorant could think that if you work long enough in a funeral parlor you stop being affected by what goes on there. It's actually quite the opposite. At least with me. The older I get, the harder it is to do my work. I've recently started considering the idea of taking early retirement as soon as I meet the qualifications. I guess I can make it through another two years and eight months. My pension will be quite a bit lower than it would be after full retirement, but I'll manage somehow. Whether I would even live to see full retirement in that job is very questionable.

I was heading for the kitchen to make something to eat when I suddenly remembered the mysterious envelope I'd left on the coffee table. I hesitated a moment, but curiosity got the better of my growling stomach. It wouldn't take long just to see what was inside. I raised the envelope to the window. Through the white paper, the rays of the afternoon sun outlined a small, dark rectangle in the middle, at somewhat of a slant. I tore open the envelope carefully on the side edge, stuck two fingers into it and took out what was there.

Even though I knew what it was right away, I stared at the movie ticket for several moments in bewilderment. Then I peered into the envelope but, as I expected, there was nothing else inside. I looked at the blue ticket again. It was valid for a screening at the Film Archives that day at six o'clock. There was no mention of what was playing. I opened my briefcase, took out the newspaper, found the movie page and looked for the program at the Film Archives. But instead of the name of the film, it said, "Closed on Monday."

I put the ticket, envelope, and newspaper on the coffee table, and then headed for the kitchen once again. It was easy to figure out what these unidentified but clever promoters were up to. They had rented the Film Archives theater for the only day it was closed to regular showings. Not a single other movie theater in town had such a convenient day off. I had had no idea that this reputable institution rented out its premises, but we live in a time of general commercialization and nothing should be surprising anymore. Even funeral services are affected, making my job all the harder.

They had sent out tickets for a series of showings to countless addresses. Certainly to many more than there were places in the theater, rightly judging that many would not respond to their invitation. Those who did get hooked by this bait would have a surprise in store for them. Instead of the film they expected, there would be some kind of dog-and-pony show. And what would be even more unusual, most of the people would stay until the end, even though they weren't the slightest bit interested in what was being offered. They might even buy it finally. It is truly unbelievable how gullible people are sometimes. I, of course, was not that way. It wasn't easy to sell me a bill of goods. In any case, even if I'd wanted to go, I would have had a hard job getting there on time. I looked at my watch: twenty-five to six. Bearing in mind the distance between my house and the Film Archives, I'd be racing against the clock.

I took a package of goulash out of the freezer and got from the cupboard the pot I use to fix frozen food. I filled the deep pot about one-third full with water and put an aluminum foil-covered brick into it. Then I put the pot on the largest burner and turned it on. I then set one end of the kitchen table with my well-practiced routine and returned to the stove. Dinner would be ready in about fifteen minutes. I spend this time every day watching the water heat up. It's not exactly exciting or useful, but what else could I do as I waited for the meal to get ready? There was no question of reading the newspaper, for example, because I never do that in the kitchen.

I'd been staring at the silver bar on the bottom for about three minutes when something suddenly snapped inside me. In a rapid succession of movements I turned off the burner, stuck my hand into the already lukewarm water and took out the package of goulash, wiped it with the dish towel hanging next to the sink and put the goulash back in the freezer. There was no time to put the pot away and clear the table. All I did was grab the two just-sliced pieces of bread from the bread basket. I started stuffing them into my mouth on my way out of the kitchen.

I picked up the ticket from the coffee table in the living room and then rushed to the vestibule. I had trouble putting on my coat. It isn't easy to pull your hand through the sleeve when you're holding a slice and a half of bread. When I finally got it through, there was a small pile of crumbs on the floor. I'd bought the bread that morning, so it was already rather dry. I was strongly tempted to clean up the mess right then and there, but I somehow managed to curb the impulse to put everything in order without delay. That could wait. I didn't have a moment to lose. I quickly put on my hat and went out. Thank God I didn't have to fool with locking the door. It was enough to close it behind me.

2

I reached the Film Archives at seven minutes after six.

The rush had truly been hectic, but that was far from the worst. I felt that everyone I met along the way gave me quizzical and suspicious looks. As I almost sprinted to catch the tram, my coat fluttering around me, holding my hat on my head with my free hand to keep it from blowing away, one of my neighbors who happened to be in the street near our building watched me in amazement. I managed to smile at him and raise my hat in greeting as I passed, but this did nothing to change the expression on his face.

Then, on the rear platform of the tram, everyone's attention was drawn to the seemingly polished gentleman as he ravenously chewed dry bread. And when I started to hiccup loudly, several heads turned away from me in disgust. It didn't help a bit when I put my hand over my mouth, held my breath and closed my nose with my thumb and index finger. I wanted to apologize to all the passengers for this unseemly behavior and explain what was going on, but as I was choosing the right words, we reached my stop.

Finally, my patience gave out and I ran across a busy street against the light, almost causing two cars to collide with a squeal of brakes. After me, along with the honking, echoed the reprimanding voice of a woman. She was standing on the other side with two small children, waiting to cross the street when the light turned green: "What an example to set for the children!" The guilty feelings that engulfed me were only somewhat assuaged by the fact that the stunt I'd just pulled had finally put an end to my hiccups.

There was one good thing about the rush and its accompanying embarrassments. Preoccupied with it all, I hadn't had time to examine my actions; questions were therefore not raised that I could and should have asked myself. What in the world was I doing? Was this how a sober, serious and self-respecting man acted? Instead of having a calm meal at home and then taking a well-deserved rest, I was rushing about heedlessly, my stomach empty, making a fool of myself right and left, in order to make it to some promotional presentation that I knew nothing about and that would most likely not interest me in the least. Such rash behavior wasn't like me at all. But just like the mess I'd left behind me in the apartment, I'd have to deal with these questions later.

A uniformed doorman was standing in front of the Film Archives. He was a short, stocky man, somewhere in his fifties. I was afraid he would greet the latecomer with a frown, but his ruddy face broke into a smile. Why, of course, this was not a normal screening where it was quite inconsiderate to the other filmgoers not to arrive on time, rather a presentation where you were welcomed no matter when you arrived.

"Excuse me, I'm a little late," I said even so, hunting through my coat pockets for the ticket.

"Not at all, not at all," replied the doorman obligingly. "We certainly wouldn't have started without you." He motioned me inside with a wave of his hand, without

11

waiting for me to show the ticket. I might as well have left it at home. No doubt he greeted every guest with the same smooth talk.

I entered the empty foyer. The other viewers who had arrived on time were already in the auditorium. As I looked around, I noticed something new. The last time I'd been there, quite some time ago, the walls hadn't been almost completely covered with photographs of film stars. Other people might not pay attention to something like that, but with me it was a professional routine. As my eyes skimmed over the pictures, I noted that under each one, along with the star's name, was their year of birth and death, like on a tombstone. The cheerful faces of the dead were turned towards me from all directions. This must be a prerequisite to having one's picture here, I concluded. Archives, like cemeteries, were places where records were kept.

As I went towards one of the two heavy, dark-red velvet curtains that covered the entrances to the auditorium, it occurred to me that my late arrival was actually rather convenient. Others in my building must have acted as rashly as I and come here. If we were to meet, it would be awkward for everyone. I would find a place somewhere in the last row in order to remain as inconspicuous as possible and be among the first to leave the auditorium when it was over. Hopefully there would still be a free seat somewhere in the back.

And there was. Actually, there were as many free seats as you could possibly wish. To be precise, in the whole auditorium only one place was taken. A woman was sitting approximately in the middle; owing to her navy blue suit, she looked like a dark, solitary island in the middle of a calmly swelling wine-colored sea. She was also wearing a wide-brimmed navy blue hat. The first thought that crossed my mind was that this was actually a blessing in disguise. At least there would be no one to witness my humiliation. How could I have been so naïve! I might have had an easier time, however, if at least one of my neighbors had come as well. Shared humiliation is somehow easier to bear.

There was no reason for me to stay there. In any case, when the organizers saw how many people they'd attracted, they'd cancel the presentation. I started to turn towards the velvet curtain and make my exit when I was stopped by a voice that made me flinch.

"May I help you?" said the usherette, taking the ticket out of my hand; as I crossed the foyer I had finally found it in my coat pocket. I hadn't noticed her before. She was standing next to the entrance, leaning against the wall, a flashlight in her hand. She was a willowy girl with short hair and large spectacles, dressed like the doorman in a dark-red uniform, the prevailing color in the Film Archives. She looked at the ticket, then headed towards the left-hand side saying, "This way, please."

What else could I do but follow her? Circumstances sometimes make a man act against his will. If I hadn't followed her, I would have been obliged to offer some sort of explanation for refusing. Regardless of how appropriate it was, I'd still feel ill at ease, and probably the girl would too. It wasn't her fault that the presentation was a failure. She was just doing her job. In any case, what did it cost to stay a little longer? Someone

13

would certainly appear to cancel the presentation. The two visitors might even get a consolation prize as a token of gratitude.

The usherette stopped at the row where the woman in navy blue was sitting and pointed her flashlight at the seat next to hers. I looked at the usherette in bewilderment. She noticed this and showed me the ticket by way of explanation. It really did say "Row 17, seat 9." Since the matter had been settled, there was no reason for her to remain any longer, so she headed back to the entrance. I stood there hesitating for a few moments and then slowly shrugged my shoulders and went towards my seat.

When I got there, I realized that I couldn't sit down just like that. If there had been other people in the auditorium, it would have been presumptuous and even impolite to address a woman who hadn't been introduced to me. Under these circumstances, however, what with our being alone, it would be discourteous to sit so close to her without saying a word. She might interpret it as a sign of bad manners or impudence. I therefore took off my hat and bowed slightly.

"Hello," I said, unable to think of anything more intelligent at such short notice.

She raised her head a little towards me and slowly nodded, then turned forward again. Most of her face was hidden by the hat brim. I caught only a glimpse of the gentle curve of her chin. Even so, this was enough to conclude that she must be a young woman. Probably beautiful, too. I took off my coat, folded it and laid it on my lap after sitting down, thinking I had to find a way to get a better look at her. As discreetly as possible, of course. I certainly didn't want to create the impression of an ill-mannered pest.

I didn't have a chance, however. As soon as I sat down, the lights in the auditorium went off. Suddenly we were in total darkness. I waited for what was to come, but nothing happened. I turned around in confusion. All I saw behind me were two small red lights above the exit, resembling the widely spaced eyes of a malevolent creature lurking in the shadows. I felt obliged to say something calming to the lady next to me. She must have been frightened. Certainly she couldn't be at ease sitting next to an unknown man in a dark, empty auditorium. To be sure, the usherette was standing somewhere in the back, but maybe she wasn't. What if she had gone out into the foyer?

As I was pondering how to address her without alarming her even more, I became aware of something that I might have overlooked had my senses of sight and hearing been engaged. Instead, in the pitch black and dead silence, my nostrils distinguished a delicate fragrance emanating from my right. For some reason I knew at once it was the extract of a flower, but I couldn't recognize which one. That was strange, since the nature of my work puts me in daily contact with all kinds of flowers. It was a soft and velvety fragrance with a certain intoxicating quality.

There was no time to dwell on this dilemma because the show was starting. What did this mean? Despite everything, had the promoters decided to make their presentation to only two viewers? That seemed to me like a pure waste of time and effort, but they might have had a different perspective with regard to the whole affair. Since they'd rented the auditorium, they might as well go ahead with the presentation. They probably figured that canceling it would be an even greater failure. For some reason I'd expected to see a master of ceremonies with assistants and stage props for a live presentation, but I'd clearly misjudged. Though indeed, this might still happen after they first showed the introductory promotional film.

If what they started to show was a promotional film, then it certainly wasn't a typical one. There were no rapidly changing scenes that made your head spin and no music with a beat so fast that it couldn't be distinguished from noise—all the characteristics that got terribly on my nerves and made me avoid watching commercials whenever I could. The screen showed the exact opposite: only one motionless scene where nothing was happening. The music matched it: a languid piano composition, similar to the murmuring of a mountain stream, as if it came from the CD compilation I listen to when I relax in front of the aquarium.

Most of the screen was taken up by a bench in a park. To the right of the bench was a streetlight, and a rather large bush dotted with big pink flowers filled the background. Judging by the luxuriant greenery and bright sunlight, this had been taken on a clear summer day. This was soon confirmed when an older woman with a shaggy dog on a leash entered the scene from the left. She was wearing a lightweight, short-sleeved dress in vivid colors, and oval-framed sunglasses. Her walk, however, was unnatural. The shot was filmed in slow motion, making it seem as though the woman and her dog were gracefully gliding across the screen, almost floating. It took them quite a while to cross the screen's short distance and leave on the right-hand side.

Then for a while nothing disturbed the uneventful scene of the bench. This would have irritated fans of action movies, but I found it quite pleasant. I felt like I do at home when I watch the dreamy, slow dance of the little fish. As the minutes passed, the daily stress I had accumulated, only increased by the headlong rush to the Film Archives, started to subside. Then I scolded myself for being selfish. After all, I wasn't at home alone, but in a movie theater next to a lady whose affinities I knew nothing about. What if she didn't like any of this, what if she would have preferred something livelier? I, of course, bore no responsibility for what was being shown, but it would have been unfeeling if I were to display any interest in it, even if no one could see me in the dark theater.

The scene finally came to life again. The figure of a small, middle-aged man appeared from the right. He was wearing a dark suit, white shirt, and black tie. He also moved in slow motion, but unlike the woman with the dog, his steps were somehow awkward, almost grotesque. He went up to the bench, sat at the end next to the streetlamp, took off his jacket and draped it across the back of the bench. Then he opened the book he had brought and settled down to read. Sitting there without moving, he appeared fused with the bench.

I watched him for a good half a minute before the realization finally hit me like a flash of lightning. I almost jumped in my seat, but was immediately over-come by a feeling of discomfort at this reaction. What would the lady think of me? There was something more important than that, however. I reproached myself for my lack of intuition, even though there were extenuating circumstances. Sometimes the most familiar thing is the hardest of all to recognize. I should have realized imme-diately which bench this was, of course. I sit on it almost every day during my lunch break, weather permitting. I approach it, however, from the side path and not from the front, because it faces a stretch of lawn where walk-ing is not permitted and thus the bench can't be reached from that side.

All right, maybe I didn't have to recognize the bench right away. When it comes down to it, they all resemble each other. The streetlight and bush did make it some-what distinctive, it's true, but I had never had any reason to pay attention to them. So far as my powers of observa-tion were concerned, they might as well not have been there. But the fact that I hadn't immediately recognized myself was already worrying. I had to think good and hard to find at least an explanation if not an excuse. I'd never seen myself on film before. I didn't even have many photographs of myself and they were primarily from my youth. I only came face to face with myself in the morn-ing when I shaved, but that was something altogether different. I knew what to expect when I looked into the mirror.

Disturbing questions began to swarm through my head, but I didn't have time to concentrate on a single one because something was happening on the screen once more. A woman approached the bench from the left and settled on the end opposite me. I first thought how strange it was: I hadn't seen her face at all and had only glanced at her briefly once before, but even so I knew at once that it was she, while it had taken quite a bit longer to recognize my own self, someone I see every day. Her bowed head was concealed by the hat brim so this time I didn't even see the delicate curve of her chin. Everything she was wearing was black, not navy blue, yet there wasn't even a shadow of a doubt: it was the lady whose undeniable presence I felt right next to me.

It wasn't only her appearance that was unusual. She moved in a different way, or rather what was unusual was that she moved normally and not in slow motion. I first thought that the entire film had gone from slow motion to normal speed, but I was wrong. It seemed to take forever to turn the pages of the book I was reading and during that time she swiftly took off her lace gloves and crossed her hands in her lap. It was as though we were in two parallel time frames that coursed at different speeds.

I didn't remember this meeting. When I become engrossed in reading, the world around me almost ceases to exist. If the lady had only passed by the bench, it wouldn't have been very surprising for me to miss her. But how could I have failed to notice her when she sat down? True, the bench was rather long, but does that explain my failure? The fact that this oversight had occurred was highly unpleasant. What more reliable symptom of aging is there than failing to notice such a person when they join you on a park bench?

She, however, noticed me. She sat there, staring straight ahead for some time, her head bowed, then unexpectedly turned towards me. During this movement, the hat brim fluttered up for a moment, revealing her profile. My initial conjecture was fully confirmed. It was one of the prettiest female faces I had ever seen. I regretted the fact that she wasn't shown in slow motion too. This revelation would then last a bit longer. A concerted effort was required to resist the temptation to look at the original next to me. Perhaps it would go unnoticed if I turned to look at her in the shadows, but I didn't dare take the risk. In any case, a gentleman never does anything in secret. Hopefully after the show I would get a chance to look at her in a way that wouldn't make me look bad.

Her head was still turned towards me. Usually a lady doesn't look so conspicuously at a complete stranger, unless there's a good reason for it. What could there have been to arouse the interest of such an individual in someone like me? Particularly since all I did was stare idiotically at the book in front of me. No coherent explanation crossed my mind. I actually know very little about women. I haven't had many opportunities to get to know them better. In any case, regardless of her motives, I was certainly flattered by the attention she gave me.

I couldn't expect this attention to last forever, of course. The lady in black finally turned her eyes away from me and concentrated on putting on her gloves. I was glad that I couldn't see her face just then. I wouldn't have enjoyed the expression of disappointment and exasperation at my behavior that must have been there. Then she got up and walked in front of the bench. She passed by me, without turning, and soon left the shot. I was alone once again, exactly like the statue of a steadfast reader, unaware of what I had just missed.

Music announced the end of the showing. The murmuring stream rose to the sound of rapids, then to the roaring of a torrent and finally to the rumble of a waterfall, and then suddenly went silent. The picture disappeared at the same time as the sound. Just as there had been no opening credits, there were none at the end. There was a fadeout and the scene in the park vanished from the screen, briefly leaving behind the afterimage of the picture. When it went out, we were in darkness once more.

Again my expectations were unfulfilled. In movie theaters the lights go on as soon as the closing credits begin. That always infuriates me because the viewers stand up right away as though in a hurry to get somewhere, and I can hardly ever see the information about the film that interests me. Now the opposite occurred. No one turned on the lights. I stayed patiently in my seat, waiting for this to happen, but the wait got longer and longer. I thought once again that I would have to take matters in hand instead of sitting there helplessly, but now, after what I'd just seen on the screen, I had even less idea than before what to say to the lady next to me. I turned towards the rear, hoping to make out the usherette standing beneath one of the exit lights. She was nowhere to be seen, and neither were the red eyes of the creature in the shadows. This time the darkness was literally complete.

The lights flashed on as I was turning back. They must have been considerably stronger than before the showing because they blinded me for a moment. My pupils quickly adjusted, however, and I could see around me once again. But there was nothing to see. Or to be exact, there was nobody to see. The seat to my right was empty. I got up slowly and turned this way and that. I was completely alone in the Film Archives auditorium.

3

As I was getting up, holding my coat and hat, something slipped off my lap onto the floor. After looking around, I bent down and picked up a white envelope. It had the same shape as the one I found in the door when I got back from work. There was no writing on this one either. How had it reached my lap? The only explanation was that the woman in navy blue had put it there before mysteriously disappearing while we were hemmed in by the dark. Needless to say I wondered why, but that brought with it a string of other questions, and this wasn't the right place to consider them. Although the auditorium was brightly lit, this didn't do much to decrease the feeling of anxiety that had come over me. I wanted to get out of there as soon as possible. After all, who stays in a movie theater after the show?

I put on my coat and hat as I got out of the row, then briskly headed for the exit. When I reached for the velvet curtain, I was suddenly struck by the fear that I would find an obstacle there. I jerked it open more vigorously than I would have done in normal circumstances. Behind it was the spacious foyer. I entered it with relief and stopped, taking everything in with a glance. There wasn't a trace of the usherette or doorman, only the multitude of eyes staring at me from the walls. As an undertaker, I understandably have no aversion to the dead, but these innocuous, smiling faces nonetheless prompted me to continue on my way without further hesitation. I felt their eyes on me through the glass entrance door even when I was out in the street, so I rushed to get out of their sight.

I generally don't like crowds, and try to stay away from places where there are lots of people. Now, however, I was glad to be part of the mass of people walking up and down the wide street. I had already gone some distance from the Film Archives when I realized that I was walking aimlessly. This wasn't the way to my apartment. But what would I do if I was to go back there? The thought of the fish as my only company wasn't appealing. On the other hand, the people around me were already starting to make me nervous. Surrounded by them, I was unable to marshal my thoughts. Why not go somewhere so I wouldn't be alone, but where it wasn't quite as noisy and congested?

My stomach decided where I would go. The two slices of bread I'd eaten on my way had only somewhat assuaged my hunger. Passing by a fast-food stand that suddenly engulfed me in strong smells, I felt dizzy. I had to eat something as soon as possible. I certainly couldn't eat out there in the street. After the embarrassing situation in the tram, eating in the street seemed quite unappealing. And it wouldn't give me the peace I wanted. The best thing would be to go to a restaurant, although it would be more expensive.

I came across one a little farther down the street. I decided to go inside when I looked through the window and saw that only two of the dozen tables were occupied. I sat as far away as I could from the others and ordered vegetable soup, two sandwiches, and mineral water. It wasn't until the waiter left that I realized why he'd given me a suspicious look. Indeed, there was no reason to sit there in my coat and hat. I put my hat on the chair next to me. When I started to take off my coat, something rustled in the sleeve. I pulled out my hand and noticed that I was holding the envelope that I'd picked up off the movie theater floor. This pulling things unnecessarily through my sleeve was already turning into a bad habit. At least the envelope didn't crumple. I put my coat over the back of the chair with my hat, then placed the envelope on a corner of the table. It could wait. I still hadn't managed to cope with what had happened after I opened the first one.

The thick, hot soup had almost disappeared from the bowl in front of me when I abruptly stopped the spoon in midair. It suddenly dawned on me. My mind always works better when I eat something hot. Of course! All at once everything fit together perfectly. There were no longer any dilemmas, puzzling questions, or secrets. The simple explanation had been staring me in the face from the very beginning, but I'd been blind to it. The people who were behind the whole thing probably counted on my being blind to the obvious. How else would their ploys ever succeed? Dear God, what a fool I was! They certainly must have had great fun from the very beginning, watching my reactions. It wasn't the least bit consoling to know that many people before me had gone through the same thing with a hidden camera.

I put the full spoonful back into the bowl. It wasn't hard to reconstruct the sequence of events. Everything had started in the park. They must have singled me out as a candidate when they noticed that I go to the same bench almost every day and spend about forty-five minutes absorbed in reading. They are constantly searching for victims, and I certainly must have seemed ideal. Indeed, would any other male but me continue to stare indifferently at a book after such a lady had sat down next to him, and then started scrutinizing him so conspicuously? I couldn't figure out where they'd managed to place the camera in the clearing in front of me, but it had certainly presented no problem. They were clever and experienced professionals. It was also unclear to me how they managed to give the impression of two speeds of movement, but I'm not at all familiar with film tricks. With the special effects that are used today it didn't have to be something out of the ordinary.

Then they followed me and found out where I live. I was the only one who received the envelope with a ticket to the movies, not all the tenants in my building as I had incorrectly concluded, assuming that it was some kind of promotional material. How could they be so sure I would accept the invitation? They probably weren't, but had taken the risk. It turned out not to be such a big risk. In that line of work you have to have an excellent grasp of psychology, and if they had been spying on me for two-and-a-half months, as I suspected, which was approximately the amount of time that had passed since the scene in the park had been filmed, they undoubtedly knew me well enough to conclude that I would probably take the bait. In this regard, I'm no great exception. Credulity is quite a widespread human trait.

The fact that they hadn't used an ordinary hidden camera but had developed a more enterprising project showed how much time they'd spent on me. Perhaps I should have been flattered by that, but my outrage wouldn't let me. The incident in the park still seemed rather unreal, as though someone else had been there and not I, but what I'd just gone through at the Film Archives weighed on me terribly. They had certainly filmed that. The funniest part was how I acted during the screening and in the dark. It was naïve to hope that I'd been protected by the lack of light. They certainly had equipment to film in total darkness.

And then a thought crossed my mind that almost made me shudder. Who could guarantee that the whole thing was over? No one. People who organize hidden cameras always show themselves in the end. The fact that they hadn't shown up meant only one thing: the show was still going on. Of course! They don't get involved in long-term projects for just two scenes. Perhaps they were secretly filming me right now and having a good laugh, seeing me petrified like this. I looked around the restaurant but I didn't notice anything unusual. The patrons at the two distant tables were concentrating on their meals and the waiter was talking to the barman. No one was paying any attention to me. But it always looks like that . . .

I continued eating my soup, bending over my bowl a bit. I couldn't let paranoia get the upper hand. Of course no one was secretly filming me now. Preparations were needed for that and there had been no time. They certainly couldn't have known that I'd be here. I had chosen the restaurant completely at random. But the respite was only temporary. A new scene undoubtedly awaited me. It was only a matter of when and where. Swallowing the last spoonful of soup, I stared blankly straight ahead, lost in thought. The answer was there before my eyes but it took some time for me to realize it.

I picked up the envelope. It was a bit heavier than the previous one. I tore it open along one end and withdrew the contents. This time it wasn't a movie ticket but what looked at first glance like some kind of formal invitation. It turned out not to be formal, but it was some sort of invitation. The stiff, fancy paper was printed with the words: Ex Libris secondhand bookstore, 36 B Chestnut Street, 7:00 PM. I turned the card over but there was nothing on the back.

Here were the time and place of the new scene. The same mysterious sparsity. They probably figured that if it had worked the first time, it certainly would work again. Why change the bait that fish have been shown to bite? But what if the fish got wise in the meantime? It seemed that the admirable experts in psychology hadn't taken into consideration the possibility that I might catch on to their game. This was quite insulting. Well, they would get an unpleasant surprise when the victim didn't show up and all their trouble was for nothing. They could fool a man once—not counting the park—but only a numbskull would allow them to do it a second time.

I laid my spoon in the empty bowl. Hey, maybe I could pay them back in kind. Maybe I could fool them a little. I'm not at all the vengeful type, but here my conscience wouldn't bother me in the least. People who film

28

with a hidden camera deserve to have the tables turned sometime. They clearly didn't suspect that I had caught on. I would go to the bookstore but wouldn't act as they expected. I would accept whatever they concocted as something quite natural. Not a single sensation would fill me with wonder, frighten, or surprise me. Let's see how they liked that.

I glanced at my watch. Eighteen minutes to seven. If I was truly supposed to reach the secondhand bookstore on time—although it wasn't clear why this was essential—then I had to act hastily again, and this was not a welcome thought. First of all, I'd gone without my dinner for that very reason. In addition, how could I reach Chestnut Street in such a short time? It was on the other side of town. Hurrying to the Film Archives, I hadn't taken a taxi because I would have been stuck in the afternoon rush hour. The tram was the fastest means of transportation then. From here to the secondhand bookstore, however, there was no direct line. I'd have to change trams and certainly wouldn't reach my destination in less than three-quarters of an hour. Now, indeed, traffic was lighter, so that with a bit of luck I could get there by taxi exactly at seven or a few minutes after. But did my desire for revenge justify the money I'd have to spend on the trip? Taxis aren't cheap and this dinner in the restaurant was already an unplanned expense. No, the best thing would be simply to forget the whole thing. I would finish my meal in peace and then head slowly for home. The long walk in fresh air would do me good.

The waiter came up to me, picked up my soup bowl and replaced it with two sandwiches on a plate. He had turned to go back to the bar when I suddenly addressed him, rising quickly.

"The bill, please. I'm in a hurry."

He gave me a strange look but didn't say a thing. He headed for the cash register, although not with much enthusiasm. I took the sandwiches and wrapped them in a napkin. I put on my hat and picked up my coat from the back of the chair. It dawned on me at the last moment that I didn't have to pull something needlessly through my coat sleeve for the third time that day. I put the wrapped sandwiches on the table, put on my coat, then put them in the wide pocket. As the waiter slowly approached with the bill, I filled a glass to the brim with mineral water and drank it. I only drink water at the end of the meal, and I wasn't thirsty after the soup, but I'd paid too much for it to leave it there. I glanced at the bill, took out a banknote that was the closest larger amount, pushed it into his hand and rushed out of the restaurant without waiting for the change. The waiter mumbled something after me, but it didn't sound much like an eager show of gratitude.

The rush saved me once again from difficult questions. But even if this had not been the case and I had to offer some explanation for my perverse decision, I doubt I would have been completely honest with myself. I would probably resort to less important reasons. I could think up at least a few: if I missed the chance to outsmart those who considered me a gullible victim, then I'd only be agreeing that their evaluation had been basically correct. Retreating like this before my opponent would start to weigh on me and might even hound me. I would accuse myself of having given way like a coward when I should have accepted the duel. Also, a man cannot always economize. Sometimes he has to pull out all the stops, regardless of the cost. Afterwards I'd have to be frugal, but what did it matter?

These would be sufficient to silence the voice of reason inside me, so I wouldn't have to pull out the last, crucial motive that was hardest to admit. Had I gone home and not to the secondhand bookstore, there would have been no hope of seeing once again what I'd only caught sight of briefly on the screen in the Film Archives: what was hidden underneath the wide hat brim.

4

Going out into the street, I was afraid I'd have to wait a long time before I found a taxi. Indeed, I rarely take them, but I do recall that every time I have needed one they were nowhere to be seen. I therefore stared in disbelief at the yellow vehicle that pulled up to the curb, right in front of the restaurant. The illuminated sign on the roof indicated that the taxi was free. Such synchronized action couldn't have been expected even after ordering a taxi from the restaurant. There are those who might have sensed some deeper meaning in this, but it was pure coincidence, of course. Sometimes you're lucky and sometimes you're not. Unlike other occasions, luck was now on my side. When things start to go your way, it's best not to get caught up in the details. Although it wouldn't hurt to think about them from time to time.

There was no time to think about anything, however. Fearful that someone else might grab it before I did, I ran up to the taxi, opened the back door and jumped into the back seat. The driver hit the gas pedal almost at the same instant, just as I was closing the door, without waiting for me to tell him where I wanted to go. The good thing about taxi drivers is that you don't have to tell them you're in a hurry. It's clear to them that you aren't sitting in their car for a leisurely drive through town. We merged into the dense flow of traffic.

"Chestnut Street, 36 B," I said to the driver, glancing into the rearview mirror in front of him. Since it had already grown quite dark, all I saw there was the silhouette of his head. He gave a brief nod when he realized I was looking at him. It seemed as though I'd hit upon one of those silent taxi drivers, which was fine with me. I don't enjoy carrying on meaningless conversations with strangers. Another good thing was that we were going in the right direction, so we didn't have to waste several minutes turning around the block. If no difficulties arose, I might still get there on time.

I wasn't very interested in watching the early evening panorama of city streets, so I wondered how to get the most use out of the next twenty minutes or so in the taxi. Ideally, of course, I would ready myself for the new hidden camera scene, but since I didn't have any idea of what lay in store for me, I didn't know how to prepare. I would have to keep my wits about me. The most important thing was to figure out the scam as soon as possible. What were their motives for choosing this particular store dealing in old books and not another? As far as I knew, nothing set it apart from the other secondhand stores that filled the neighborhood. I thought I'd gone into it once or twice, but could hardly remember it. I could even be mixing it up with another store, although I still thought I'd been in the Ex Libris. In any case, that had been long ago, considerably before these people took an interest in me, so my earlier visits had nothing to do with their choice.

I stuck my hands in my coat pockets without thinking and touched the napkin in the right one. I felt something gooey and sticky on my fingertips. Apparently I hadn't wrapped the sandwiches very well. I took the little bundle out of my pocket and in the faint light noticed that some sort of spread, probably mayonnaise, had leaked through the porous paper. I wiped my fingers on the clean part of the napkin and then stuck my hand back in. There was mayonnaise inside the pocket too. That was all I needed. It would be awful if the stain had gone through the lining. Just when there was going to be more filming. I would look even more comical than usual. I touched the outside of my coat and sighed with relief on discovering that there was no stain. I took out my handkerchief, carefully turned the pocket inside out and wiped the soiled part. That was only a temporary solution to the problem. Even though the mess couldn't be seen, I'd have to have the coat dry-cleaned. I couldn't wear it like that, could I? Another expense. This adventure was costing me more and more; it served me right for not knowing when to stop. Maybe I could ask the organizers to pay for the damage. All of this was taking place without my consent. But what kind of hidden camera would it be if they made the film with the victim's consent?

Putting the sandwiches back in my pocket was out of the question. I hesitated for a moment, considering what to do with them. There was an ashtray on the inside of the door, but it was too small. I could ask the driver to get rid of them somehow—he might have a bigger ashtray up front or even a wastebasket—but then I'd have to go into a complicated explanation and I didn't feel up to it. I thought of simply leaving the leaking bundle unnoticed on the seat next to me, or even better, on the floor, but was instantly ashamed of myself. I, who was horrified when other people did such things, was I to follow their example? In the end, there was only one way to get rid of the sandwiches for good. It was simple, quick, and safe, although not completely without its drawbacks. But nothing's perfect.

I moved from the middle of the seat where I'd been sitting, all the way to the left-hand door. The rearview mirror was outside my field of vision, which meant that the driver couldn't see me anymore. Just in case, I bent down a bit behind the back of his seat, then took a bite. I don't usually smack my lips when I eat, so the taxi driver certainly couldn't hear me, but even so I did my best to chew as little as possible. It would have been most unfortunate if some careless noise were to give me away. Eating while riding in a taxi might even be prohibited for all I knew. I don't know what I would have done if the driver caught me in the act, but it wouldn't be good if he asked me to leave the taxi.

And then a piece got stuck at the back of my throat. I barely managed to prevent myself from choking. What if the incident in the tram recurred? Gulping down half-chewed mouthfuls was almost certain to bring on an attack of hiccupping. It would be a very audible *corpus delicti*. I returned the piece to the front of my mouth and chopped it up frantically with my teeth, no longer worried that the noise might reach the driver's ears. Compared to hiccupping, it was a minor sound. Now a bit of mineral water was what I really needed, but I'd pointlessly gulped down a full glass in the restaurant. Whoever would have thought I'd need it in a taxi? But what else could I have done? Poured the water back into the bottle, hidden it in my other coat pocket and taken it out of the restaurant? That would only have exposed me to the embarrassment of the waiter running after me and accusing me of stealing the inventory. Or worse still, if I got past the waiter, what if the bottle, which was without a cap, spilled in my pocket? Then I'd have had a great deal more trouble than with the mayonnaise. When I got out of the taxi and the driver saw that I was wet from the waist down, and that there was a puddle behind me on the seat, who knows what might have crossed his mind.

Pulled suddenly to the right by the taxi turning, I once again found myself in the taxi driver's field of vision. But I didn't have to fear that he would catch me with the sandwiches. His attention was focused on the road ahead. The traffic had thinned a little when we entered a wide boulevard and he'd taken immediate advantage of it. He had turned sharply into the left-hand lane, ignoring the angry honking from the car he'd cut off. He stayed there briefly, then pulled a similar maneuver back again, this time accompanied not only by honking but headlights flashing in protest from other cars. This returned me to my previous position.

If I didn't want to fly from one side of the seat to the other, I'd have to put the sandwiches in one hand and hold onto the handle above the door with the other. It would be even safer if I put on my seatbelt, but I hadn't been able to find it during the wild ride, and it didn't seem appropriate to bother the driver just then with my question. The man was making a wholehearted effort to get me to the address as soon as possible, even greater than was to be expected from a dedicated taxi driver, particularly since I hadn't got around to telling him that I was in a hurry.

Driving along the boulevard turned into a real slalom, with squealing tires, sharp swerves, collisions avoided by a hair and sudden braking. I don't even like watching reckless driving in movies; without the slightest personal experience I could imagine how unpleasant it was. And now I was seeing for myself. I gripped the handle so firmly that I thought it would break off in my hand any minute. Finishing the sandwiches was quite out of the question. Eating might make me nauseous, like getting seasick on a ship, and I wasn't at all sure I'd be able to find my mouth. I avoided looking ahead because it only made me feel worse.

How in the world had I come to deserve this? Fair enough, I'd decided to take up the gauntlet, but I didn't have to accept the pace they were forcing on me. That had been clear back at the Film Archives. Hadn't the doorman said they certainly wouldn't start without me? How could they, anyway? I was their main actor. And now that I was onto their game, instead of acting like a star, maybe even a spoiled one, giving them a bit of a headache, here I was working my tail off like some third-rate extra. I was risking my life to reach some secondhand bookstore at the appointed time. Who rushes to a used bookstore? You couldn't be late for anything there.

I was just about to ask the driver to slow down—we could have had an accident, plus there was a good chance we'd be stopped by the police, and any encounter with them wouldn't be of short duration—when he did so of his own accord. He turned down a side street where there was almost no traffic. Then, instead of hitting the gas with no one blocking him, he continued at a normal speed. Who can figure out taxi drivers? There must be some oddballs among them. Maybe I'd run into a guy who got a kick out of driving recklessly, but only on boulevards. It was a good thing I didn't use their services very often.

Although it was safe to let go of the handle now, I didn't. My hand seemed to have fused with it. Nor did I continue eating my sandwiches. My stomach was still all topsy-turvy. The driver would see me holding them when I got out of the car, but it no longer mattered. I would have loved to hear him criticize me for that. Then there'd be nothing to stop me from telling him just what I thought about his driving.

I didn't know this part of town very well, particularly not in the dark, so I couldn't tell how much farther we had to go. Judging by the time spent in the taxi, it couldn't be very much. Indeed, two more turns brought us to Chestnut Street. The old trees it was named after lined the street on both sides. Behind them were rows of shop windows filled with the past. It had no lack of admirers; quite a few people were inside the second-hand shops and in front of them.

The taxi stopped outside the Ex Libris bookstore. I recognized it as soon as I saw it through the car window. I'd been there before and suddenly remembered the book I'd bought. Unfortunately, I hadn't had much use for the illustrated guide entitled *You and Your Tropical*

Fish. Although still a beginner at the time, I already knew most of the practical advice the author gave about maintaining an aquarium. But since the price had been cheap even for me, I didn't feel too bad about the fact that it was useless. If it hadn't been a book, I might have gotten rid of it. As it was, I'd put it on the bookshelf and forgotten about it.

I got out of the taxi without trying to hide what remained of the sandwiches. I turned towards the driver's window to ask what I owed him, but he spoke before I had a chance.

"I hope you're satisfied. We got here on time, didn't we?"

His unexpected question confused me, so I reacted spontaneously. I glanced at my watch and saw that it was indeed a minute-and-a-half to seven. I was just about to agree and thank him, regardless of the wild ride down the boulevard, when alarm bells went off in my head. How did he know that I was supposed to be here by a certain time? I hadn't mentioned it to him. In addition, his voice sounded familiar. I'd heard it somewhere before. Quite recently.

I looked hard at the figure behind the lowered front window. The man was wearing the brown uniform of a taxi driver, with a cap of the same color. He also had a broad mustache. This disguise, however, wasn't enough to deceive me. It took considerable effort to keep from showing my surprise.

"Yes, on time," I replied to the doorman who had greeted me at the Film Archives less than an hour ago.

The taxi driver smiled, raised two fingers to the brim of his cap, touched it, then started the car. I stood there on the curb, watching him drive off down Chestnut Street.

So much for the taxi appearing right when I needed it. How could I have believed this; I've never had a stroke of luck my whole life. And then assuming that the oddball nature of a taxi driver was behind the wild drive down the boulevard. Unforgivably naïve. My behavior in the back seat would end up being the centerpiece of this hidden camera episode. It even outdid silent slapstick comedy. I was completely embarrassed. The only way I could go on now was to turn over a new leaf. I had underestimated my opponent. Henceforth my eyes would be wide open, I'd take nothing for granted, I'd be suspicious of the most innocent thing. Coincidence and twists of fate no longer existed. Paranoia ruled!

As I turned around on the sidewalk, a consoling thought crossed my mind. It would have been a lot worse if, after all I'd gone through, the taxi driver had charged me for the ride. At least I'd got off lightly in that respect.

This face-saving slightly restored my self-confidence, and I headed for the entrance to the secondhand bookstore.

5

I didn't enter the bookstore right away. Standing in front of the door, I realized I was still holding what was left of the sandwiches. Of course I couldn't go in with them. I didn't want to play into their hands. The camera would certainly be running inside and they'd want to show me in the most hilarious light possible. And what was more grotesque than an ostensibly serious gentleman entering a bookstore holding a little bundle of food covered with mayonnaise? That would give the audience good reason for a new burst of laughter. I could have stayed outside a bit longer and finished the sandwiches, but I couldn't eat them in the half minute at most that remained until seven. Or rather, not eat them slowly enough to avoid getting the hiccups. It still wasn't clear to me why it was so important that I reach this place at the appointed hour. After all I'd been through in the taxi to get there on time, however, it would be quite senseless to be late because of a sandwich. I looked around and saw a litter basket close by. I put the greasy napkin into it with a feeling of defeat. For the second time that day I hadn't finished a meal. Plus, this was a sheer waste of money. I could have fixed a sumptuous meal at home for the amount I'd paid for two sandwiches in the restaurant.

There wasn't a single customer in the secondhand bookstore. At first I thought this was strange, since the other stores in the neighborhood were teeming with customers, and then I realized what was going on. The next scene, whatever it was, clearly was meant for only one actor. No extras required. How had they fixed it so no one else was there? At that time of day used bookstores have plenty of customers. What if someone wanted to come in while the shooting was going on? It was quite lively outside and people passed by the front window continually. Then again, why should I worry? That wasn't the job of the show's star. Let the organizers take care of the technical details. My job was to play the role I'd been assigned.

To the right of the entrance, at a counter with an old-fashioned cash register on the corner, a girl sat reading. She raised her head when the bells above the door jingled.

"Good evening. We stay open only until eight tonight and not until midnight as we usually do."

Her eyes returned to her book, so she didn't notice I was still looking at her. She wasn't wearing glasses and her hair seemed to be a little longer and lighter, but there was no doubt about it. Before me was the usherette from the Film Archives. There was something wrong here. If the organizers hadn't wanted me to recognize the taxi driver and salesgirl, they should have done a better job of disguising them or else brought in new actors. This looked more like changing costumes for a new scene. Unless they'd completely miscalculated my powers of observation—and I couldn't blame them for this after that embarrassment in the park—then whatever game they were playing eluded me.

This only increased the need for vigilance. I did have a certain advantage, however. They didn't know I was no longer an innocent victim dashing headlong into a new trap. On the other hand, I knew nothing about what they'd prepared for me this time. Or almost nothing. The salesgirl had just told me the store was closing in one hour. Did that mean the scene would last that long? It seemed too lengthy for a hidden camera episode. Later, during editing, they would probably cut it down to size.

Also, if the scenario was to remain true to form, I should expect a third person to appear at the places where the invitations sent me. Luckily the girl wasn't looking at me, because she would have seen me suddenly blush. I wondered if there'd be another change in the color of her suit. What came after black and navy blue? And what was the meaning of this color spectrum, if there was any?

I looked around. The place had not changed much since my visit long ago. It was much more a jumbled storeroom than a well-ordered bookstore. Three of the walls were covered ceiling to floor with shelves filled haphazardly with books; volumes of different sizes, thickness, and condition were arranged at random. They were jammed together, accentuating the cluttered impression. The bookstore was simply too small to accommodate the entire stock satisfactorily. The center of the room was filled with books piled one on top of the other. They formed a rectangle that rose up at least a meter from the floor and stayed in place owing to the fact that the columns supported each other. Between this paper island and the shelves was only an aisle so narrow that two people couldn't pass each other without getting stuck.

There was a ladder that slid on guide rails if you wanted to reach a book on the upper shelves. At the moment it was on the wall facing the entrance, next to the door leading to the back room. But that was the only help available; you were on your own in all other respects. The last time I'd been there a young salesman was sitting at the desk. He had also been reading, and smoking a pipe. I'd asked him to show me where I could find a book about maintaining an aquarium. He looked at me as though I'd asked something completely outrageous and didn't even deign to answer. He just shrugged his shoulders and indicated a wide sweep in front of him with his pipe. This was quite articulate: over there somewhere. It had taken more than one hour and forty minutes of persistent searching until I finally stumbled on what I wanted in one of the most crammed corners of the store. When it turned out soon after that my efforts had been in vain, I wasn't too worried. Long ago I'd become hardened to such bad luck. That's the story of my life.

What surprise was lying in wait for me in this sea of old books? I tried to remember the few hidden camera shows I'd watched on television. None had taken place in a used bookstore, but there was a general pattern that could fit any situation. If you wanted to make a person look funny, you had to take them outside their ordinary context. Then predicaments started to develop that seemed inexplicable or even impossible. What might those be here? Standing next to the entrance, as though on the edge of a minefield, I thought about this for a while. The two episodes I'd already been through had differed in tone. Everything had seemed polished at the Film Archives, while the humor in the taxi had been rather coarse. If the place determined the tone, then a bookstore, even one selling used books, was more suited to something low-key than to a slapstick prank.

I couldn't be sure, however. On the other hand, I couldn't keep on standing there. The girl wasn't paying any attention to me, but unless I moved pretty soon I would appear suspicious. And I didn't want them to realize I saw through them. I advanced cautiously towards the left, trying to anticipate any possible danger. Confined to the narrow aisle, the first thing that crossed my mind was that the books had been set in the middle like that so I would accidentally disturb them and the whole unsteady structure would collapse, with me buried under a pile of dusty books. I hoped this wasn't the case. It would be both unpleasant and even more degrading than the adventure in the taxi. It would dispel any sense of good taste. Even if I'd agreed to take part in a hidden camera episode, I still had the right to my self-respect.

Just to be on the safe side, I made my way slowly and tried not to brush against the hill of books. When I reached the place where the aisle made a ninety-degree turn to the right, I stopped dead in my tracks. What if I was expecting the attack from the wrong side? Perhaps the unsteady rectangle in the middle was only meant to trick me, while a whole shelf of books was about to fall on me? No. I didn't think so. Something like that would endanger not only my self-respect but my health. People get into trouble in these programs but their lives are certainly not in danger. The victims or their heirs could sue the organizers for a ton of money.

I didn't dare drop my guard. Even if my life was safe, other calamities could happen. As I continued to make my way, I tried to put myself in the organizers' shoes. What booby trap could be set up here? What if the fire sprinklers suddenly went off? No, that would cause too much damage. I'd certainly look funny all wet, but the water would ruin many of the books. These second-hand editions weren't worth much, but destroying even cheap books for the sake of a gag would seem somehow barbaric.

Maybe there was an animal waiting for me around the next corner. It didn't have to be a ferocious crocodile, lion, or shark. In any case, those couldn't fit into this cramped space. It would be enough to surprise me with an anteater, a seal, or even a common peacock, so that when I fled in panic I demolished everything around me. But that didn't seem very probable either. The Society for the Prevention of Cruelty to Animals might make a fuss about animal abuse.

When I reached the corner with the door to the back room and the ladder, I didn't turn right away. I waited a bit and then peered cautiously around the corner. The aisle was empty. Oh! It suddenly dawned on me. Had I not been aware that they were filming me, I might even have struck myself on the forehead. My thinking was all wrong, so my expectations were wrong. Nothing would collapse, there wouldn't be any sprinklers, animals or similar tricks from the inventory of common-place hidden cameras. This wasn't one of those. I wasn't just a chance passerby or visitor. I'd come there with an invitation. They probably didn't know I'd found them out, but it was clear to them I knew something was up. I'd become distrustful. The basic meaning of the show had been completely reversed. Instead of organizing a comic surprise for an unsuspecting victim, they'd made the victim a bundle of nerves in constant expectation of a practical joke. But there was no practical joke. On the contrary, everything was quite normal—except for the victim's behavior. Indeed, whoever behaved in a second-hand bookstore as if they'd suddenly landed in a jungle full of hidden danger? This type of humor wasn't the least bit coarse and primitive, rather quite refined.

Even though I was the victim, I had to congratulate them on their ingenuity. In any case, this was far more bearable than those burlesque cartwheels in the taxi. I didn't really understand why that nonsense had been necessary. It clashed with all the rest. Had the taxi driver pulled a stunt of his own to spite me a little because he only had a supporting role? No, such impulsiveness was hard to imagine. It had most likely been done to prevent me from trying to figure out what was going on. Perhaps there hadn't been any filming in the car. But even if there had, it would be an easy matter to remove it later on, like a foreign body. Now that I understood their strategy, I had to figure out what to do next. Although the role of victim was tolerable in this form, I still didn't like it. I was expected to act confused and uncertain, in constant fear that something was about to happen to me. The only way to respond to that was to behave in quite the opposite manner, like an ordinary customer who has stopped by a secondhand bookstore to check out the books on display. That's what I'd do, quite unruffled and relaxed. They could film to their heart's content. Let them be puzzled for a change.

I continued calmly down the aisle, my eyes glancing left and right. Whoever was watching me certainly must have wondered about this sudden change in attitude. I smiled to myself, not without a touch of malice. Did they have a ready-made response or was this turnabout quite unexpected? If they had one, then the girl playing the salesgirl in this scene would be the first to make a move. But while I had completed the circuit of the island and was back in front of the counter once again, she was still completely engrossed in the book before her. To all appearances she wasn't the least interested in what I was doing. That could mean only one thing: a war of nerves awaited us. Some fifty minutes remained until the second-hand bookstore closed. All right, let's see just how long they could hold out. Time wasn't on their side here.

I slowly started a new round. This time I turned towards the shelves. Although the middle was free of traps, it was still quite wobbly so I could unintentionally stumble and knock over one of the columns. That would be an unexpected bonus for the hidden cameraman, who must be slowly losing patience. I was already getting used to the narrow passage with its walls of books. If you went sideways, there was enough room in front and back. Besides, it actually made no difference which way I looked. The volumes making up the island were neither more important nor more interesting than those on the shelves. And vice versa.

After I'd made another round, I realized something was missing. I never go into a bookstore without good reason. I go into them in order to buy a specific book. That can take a brief time if the bookseller serves me quickly, or longer if I have to look for it by myself, as I'd done before in this store. I've never stopped by a store selling new or used books just to browse. Many people love to browse, but that lack of purpose soon starts to irritate me. In my line of work, you don't look kindly on killing time.

And that's just what awaited me. I hadn't come here in search of a book, so the empty three-quarters of an hour suddenly seemed quite long. Time didn't appear to be on my side, either. I might capitulate before my opponent, as they probably hoped I would. Unless, of course, I discovered some purpose to keep me occupied. Not much effort was needed to find one. It was obvious. The fact that I'd come into the secondhand bookstore without intending to buy anything could change. I would no longer go round in circles, I would set out to find a book.

What should I look for? Once again I didn't have to think very hard. The answer came of its own accord. What would be more natural under the given circumstances than to look for a book on the subject of hidden cameras? Something like that must certainly exist, given the popularity of such programs. Clearly I couldn't make any inquiries of the salesgirl. If I did and she indicated where to find such a book, I'd have to think up something else to pass the time until eight. I doubted she would tell me, though. Most likely she would shrug her shoulders like the young man with the pipe several years ago. Moreover, if I asked her for such a book I would be announcing that I was onto them. No, everything indicated that I should look for it by myself.

Things like this have to be done systematically, otherwise you can easily overlook what you're searching for, assuming it exists. If I hadn't worked that way I would never have found *You and Your Tropical Fish*. I decided to start on the left, from the first shelf next to the display window. I would commence at the bottom, working from left to right, the lowest row first, then the one above it and so on. I wouldn't be able to see the last three top rows, unfortunately. The room was quite high and I'm rather short. This method wasn't too bad, though. Seven rows were accessible, which meant I had a seventy percent chance of success. This percentage would be considerably less if the books in the middle of the room were included, but I wasn't going to count them. Even if I'd wanted to look through them, I wouldn't have time before the store closed. I wasn't even certain there would be time for this shorter shelf-based system.

I ended up making more progress than I expected. It's always easier to search when you know what you're looking for. My eyes flitted over the titles on the book spines, looking for two key words: "hidden camera." A number of the books unfortunately didn't have spines. I decided to disregard them. It would take too long to pull each one out in order to read the title on the cover, and it probably wouldn't be worth the effort. The more worn the book the older it would be, and this type of show was relatively new. Even so, I took out one or two undamaged books from the shelves. Their spines didn't contain the words "hidden camera" but the titles allowed the possibility that this was their subject. Each one turned out to be a red herring.

I'd reached approximately the middle of the wall facing the entrance when I wondered what the organizers thought about my diligent search. They certainly must be intrigued by what I was trying to find. Great. Let them get a taste of the concealment game from the other side. Then it occurred to me: this game didn't have to end in my favor. What if I did find a book on the hidden camera? I couldn't buy it. When I took it to the counter to pay for it, the girl would see what I'd chosen. It would be just like asking her where to look for it. My advantage would evaporate instantly.

What else could I do? I first thought of something quite unseemly: steal it. I would never do any such thing, of course, if I were able to obtain it legally. The salesgirl wasn't looking at me, I could slip it into my other coat pocket, the one which hadn't contained the sandwiches; it was even wide enough for a large volume. Yes, but the cameras were watching me! I'd almost overlooked that fact. Not only were they watching, they were filming me. The police would have a prime piece of evidence. What about hiding it in some out-of-the-way place, then coming back for it later? No, that wouldn't work either. They would find it easily from the footage. The situation seemed hopeless, but then a solution came to me, perfect in its simplicity. If I found such a book, I wouldn't do anything. Not a thing. I would do nothing to indicate that my search had been successful. I would take great care to remember the book's place and keep on pretending to examine the shelves. The next afternoon, when the secondhand bookstore was open as normal, I'd stop by once again and buy it. The chances were quite negligible that someone would get to it before me in the meantime.

By the time I reached the last shelf to the right of the entrance, it had grown apparent that all my cunning had been in vain. I hadn't found a single work on hidden cameras. I looked at the clock. It was twelve minutes to eight—too long to spend the time doing nothing. I had to find something to do. I looked hesitantly at the panorama of books surrounding me on all three sides, then made for the ladder in the corner diagonally opposite. I would climb up and start searching through the upper shelves. I hadn't the faintest hope that my luck would improve. All I wanted to do was to confuse my opponents further. I would take out a book with the most far-fetched title, pretend to be overjoyed at finding what I was looking for at last, then immerse myself and carefully leaf through it.

I didn't stop until my hat almost touched the ceiling. I stuck my left arm around the rung, bent my elbow and anchored myself that way. I twisted my head a bit to the side to enable me to read the titles on the spines more easily. I didn't have to look very long. Any of the works in the row before my eyes could have served the purpose. Someone seemed to have taken considerable effort to line up the most outlandish titles possible: *The Avant-Garde Art of Cannibal Communities*, *The Influence of Climate on the Puberty of Ants*, *Sports in Weightlessness for the Handicapped.* I reached for the fourth book in the row. The volumes were wedged in tightly even at this height. I had to be careful, when I pulled it out, that several others didn't come along with it, something that wasn't easy to do with just one hand. I finally extracted a thin, tattered copy, its title displayed prominently on the faded cover: *Is There Life Before Birth?* There was also a subheading: *An Essay in Prenatal Eschatology.*

As a man who has spent his whole life cremating and burying the dead, I think the absolute worst of such nonsense, and for this very reason the book was the perfect choice. It would lead them to think of me very differently. I started turning the pages, hoping the camera was filming in close-up, recording my features lit with joy. It took a great deal of effort to maintain the expression on my face, because the amateur drawings that illustrated the work made me want to laugh. I've never been able to understand people who believe in an existence other than that of this world. It's enough to take one look at the little pile of ashes that remains after the dead are cremated to lose any illusions about life beyond the grave. And this book was about something even more incoherent: life before birth. Really, prenatal eschatology!

It was very quiet in the bookstore. The sounds outside were muted and the girl was silent. The only thing that had disturbed the quiet was my movements. Now, however, I too was immobile and almost noiseless, standing at the top of the ladder. The unexpected squeak of the back-room door below jerked me out of my reverie like a sudden explosion. If I hadn't been holding onto the rung,

I might have lost my balance and plunged to the floor or onto the books in the middle. Nothing happened for several moments. And then a large purple disc-shaped object emerged from the back room and stopped briefly below me. I stared at it, not realizing what it was.

It was not until it moved once again, making its way along the aisle between the shelves and the island of books, that I realized what it was. Or rather, who it was. I almost dropped the book I was holding. The angle had tricked me. Seen from directly above, the wide-brimmed hat possessed no third dimension. In addition, even though I'd suspected there would be another change in color, I had no way of knowing that this time it would be purple. As the lady slowly made her way down the canyon of books, more and more of her outfit could be seen. I don't have a very good eye for women's fashions, so I might be mistaken, but it seemed to me that she'd been wearing the same outfit on all three occasions, except in a different color. If that were true, then the intention was to increase my bewilderment even more. What other reason could there be for this colorful fashion show of one and the same ensemble?

As though glued to the ladder, I watched the lady head towards the door. I glanced briefly at the salesgirl. She was hunched over her book, undeterred. It seemed that nothing could shake her impassivity. And that was clearly part of the plan. I was really curious as to what she would do when I left the secondhand bookstore. Would she fail to react to that too? We would find out soon enough. In any case, the salesgirl seemed to be deaf to the bells that jingled when the lady opened the door.

She went out and turned right. Her silhouette, drawn by the glow of a nearby streetlight, glided swiftly past the display window like a purple apparition.

I no longer had any reason to be up there by the ceiling. I tried to put the book back in its place, but it wasn't an easy task. In any case, who cared? I wouldn't upset anything if I put it someplace else. There wasn't any order to disturb. I put it horizontally in the narrow space above the other volumes, then quickly climbed down to the floor. I didn't move from the foot of the ladder.

Until a moment ago it had seemed I had the initiative, that I was even controlling events. Now that self-confidence vanished. I realized I needed to do something right away, but I didn't know what. Should I rush after the lady? She was already out of sight, but I still might be able to catch up with her. Yes, and then what? What could I ask her, what could I do? Wasn't this just what they expected of me? Attack an unknown lady in the street like a mugger? They would certainly have cameras outside. No, I wouldn't fall into that trap. In which case, what else remained? I couldn't just stand there until the girl behind the counter asked me to leave the store at eight o'clock.

Then my eyes fell on the door to the back room. The lady in purple had left it ajar and the light was on. The voice of reason warned me once again that this couldn't be by accident, that this too must be a trap. But I turned a deaf ear to it. Lack of time once more forced me to act. I didn't turn around to check whether the girl would see me. If she had been a real salesgirl she certainly would have objected to anyone going into a private room. This way, there was nothing to hold me back and I doubted anyone would reprimand me. On the contrary, one might say. I opened the door and went inside, then closed it behind me.

It was a small room, barely three by three meters, without a window or any other door. There was nothing inside but a table in the middle, a chair next to it and a rolltop cabinet on the right-hand side. The rough floor-boards had no covering. Under normal circumstances, this was probably where the accounting would be done. A large bulb hung from the ceiling on a long flex and brightly illuminated the table under it. The round brass shade above it left the upper part of the room in semi-darkness.

I didn't see what was on the table right away because the tall back of the chair back was hiding it. When I drew closer, I saw a rather large book on the table. It was opened approximately in the middle. A red ribbon marked the place between two pages. One glance was enough to see that this book differed from all the others in the secondhand bookstore. It was quite new.

I knew I didn't have much time and shouldn't hesitate, yet I waited several moments before acting. I tried to figure out what they were up to. The book had obviously been left on the table so that I'd find it. It was too conspicuous to be overlooked. Also, I doubted that it had been opened at some arbitrary place. Why were these two pages important? If they'd wanted me to read them, why had they left everything to the last minute? I quickly looked at my watch. It was a bit more than one minute to eight. I couldn't do it. The typeface was small and condensed. Couldn't the lady have come out a little earlier? And why, since the very beginning, had they been constantly and needlessly making me rush? Couldn't hidden camera episodes be made at a slower pace?

Were they sending me the wrong signals again? Did they want me to believe the book was opened intentionally at that place, although it wasn't true? So where should I expect the surprise? There was only one way to find out. I extended my hand cautiously and picked up the book. Nothing happened. The volume was heavy compared to its size and I could feel the fine texture of the plasticized cover's relief on my palm and fingers. My nostrils were tickled by the special smell of paper just off the press.

With unfocused eyes I closely examined the dense pattern of text, not even trying to read it, and then closed the book. The reflection off the cover's smooth surface hurt my eyes. I had to change the angle a little to avoid it—and the front cover of the book was finally visible. The background was a reproduction of a painting showing a field thickly covered with purple flowers. Three rows of words in letters of varying sizes were written over them. All the letters were a darker shade of the same color, with a black border that set them apart.

The largest was the title that took up the central part:

Hidden Camera

Underneath it, in somewhat smaller letters, was written:

A Novel

At the very bottom, in the smallest letters, was the author's name:

(My Name)

So this was the reason I'd been brought to the second-hand bookstore! I was supposed to see this book. The trap had been laid here the whole time and not in the main part of the bookstore. What I'd done there had been pointless. I'd been so certain I was leading them on and instead I'd entertained them with my awkward antics. Maybe they hadn't even been filming while I was carefully searching the shelves. I felt a shudder suddenly run up and down my spine. If they hadn't been filming out there, the cameras were certainly running now! The new scene had started the moment I entered this little room.

I couldn't let the confusion show on my face. That was just what they wanted. I had to accept with calm the existence of a book allegedly written by me, as though I really had written it. I was expected to do anything but stand there impassively. I kept my composure as I opened the cover. Without doubt the hoax was just there, on the cover. It alone had been printed and wrapped around some book of the appropriate size. They'd counted on this being more than enough. I'd be flabbergasted when I read my name and in my confusion I wouldn't check any further. I might even hurl the large volume aside as though it were contaminated.

Well, they'd miscalculated. The hoax would soon be exposed. I turned the first page—and once again had trouble hiding my surprise. Before me was one more confirmation that this hidden camera episode had been thoroughly prepared. The cover wasn't wrapped around a book that had nothing to do with it. The first page repeated the data on the cover. With one addition: the date of publication. A year that was exactly half a decade away. They'd really made an effort. They'd even taken into consideration the possibility that I might not be intimidated and would look inside the book. If I hadn't been sufficiently rattled by all the rest, this impossible year was supposed to be the coup de grâce.

But it wasn't. I don't give in that easily. The ruse might have worked thus far, but no further. Since I, of course, hadn't written this book, after the first page they'd used the work of another author. Although quite intrigued to find out who they'd chosen as my ghost writer, I didn't turn any more pages. The most important thing right then was to defeat their expectations. I shut the book apathetically as though it were a work that didn't interest me in the slightest. As I returned it to the table, I noted that the reproduction continued across the spine to the back cover. I had no reason to look at the continuation of this unchanging panorama of flowers, particularly since purple isn't one of my favorite colors. But something made me turn the book face down on the table—and I was staring right at her.

A moment later, when I was plunged into pitch blackness, my anger was stronger than this new surprise. I stared helplessly at the flickering spots that quickly faded in the opaque darkness. She was dressed exactly as she had been a moment ago, as though she hadn't left the room at all but gone straight into the picture on the back of the cover. Her head was raised so the hat brim didn't hide it, but the scene wasn't clearly defined enough to make out the details properly. What remained in my memory seemed deceptive and inconstant, as though I'd looked at a pointillist canvas through glasses with the wrong prescription. The book, luckily, was still on the table in front of me. As soon as the lights went back on, I'd finally have a chance to examine this face that was eluding me so persistently.

If they kept to the ending of the scene in the Film Archives, the light should go back on quite soon. I stood by the table, waiting for this to happen. Several minutes slowly passed before I realized that the scenario had changed. The darkness here wouldn't be dispelled. There was nothing left for me to do but turn around and head towards the invisible door. I put my hand out in front of me like a blind man. What were they up to now? Maybe they had silently locked the door from the outside and were now filming me with an infrared camera, curious to see how I coped. If this was the case, my only way out would be by force. But I wouldn't give them the pleasure of watching me break down the door. Instead, I'd announce to them in a loud voice that the show was over. I no longer wanted to participate in their hidden camera episode. Everything has its limit. I wouldn't let them make a fool out of me.

I reached the door sooner than I expected. Deprived of any help from my eyes, I hadn't properly judged the distance. I started to grope for the handle and soon found it. I pressed down, almost convinced that nothing would happen. But there was no resistance. I pulled on the door and it started to open towards me with a squeak. I opened it all the way and could finally see once again. The light had been turned off in the main shop too, but after the total darkness of the back room the feeble street light pouring in through the front window almost made me squint.

The girl was no longer behind the counter. I seemed to be the only person in the store, but could I be sure? In any case, there was nothing to keep me there anymore, so I headed for the exit, walking carefully among the books in the gloom. I was already at the door when I realized I had to go back. The book with her picture was lying on the table. I wouldn't leave without it, even if it meant falling into a new trap.

As I sidled my way back along the cramped aisle, I wondered what that trap might be. If I took the book with me and the police were waiting outside, having been informed that there was a robber in the store, I'd have a terrible time justifying my presence in there. I might make reference to the hidden camera, but who would believe me? What proof did I have? A piece of paper with the name and address of this bookstore. Really convincing. Particularly when they noticed that I was holding a book without any sort of receipt. I didn't suppose it would help very much that I was its alleged author. Not even writers are allowed to steal their own works. My only hope would be for the organizers to appear just as I was about to be arrested and clear up the whole thing, but did I dare rely on that? What if the culmination of the program was for the leading man to go to prison? That wouldn't surprise me one bit. Television today is notorious for its ruthlessness. Shows even trample over corpses to increase their viewer ratings. If they can't find real excitement that panders to the base instincts of the viewers, they think nothing of producing it themselves.

This quite obvious danger, however, did not discourage me. That's what happens when you don't go through the phase of irrational behavior at the proper time. I even felt proud of the fact that I was exposing myself to such risk because of a lady's picture. There was something almost chivalrous about it. But when I reached the open door to the back room, I realized that this feat wouldn't be an easy one. That is to say, I couldn't see a thing. My body blocked the weak light coming from the outside. Almost total darkness gaped before me once more.

I stuck out my hands and moved boldly forward. Would a knight yield before a bit of darkness? Three steps brought me to the back of the chair. I went around it and grabbed the edge of the table. I remembered approximately where I'd put the book and searched for it in that spot. But it wasn't there. I must have made a mistake. Even so, the table was small, and I'd find it in an instant. But I didn't. I groped all over the surface; there was nothing on it. Cold fingers of fear suddenly grabbed me. I could almost feel hidden eyes on me from the darkness all around. And then I did something that wasn't the least bit chivalrous. I turned and ran.

What had threatened to happen the moment I set foot inside the secondhand bookstore finally, inexorably, happened. Hurtling towards the exit, I no longer cared about the columns of books in the center. The sound of their collapsing like dominos behind me increased the impression that someone was chasing me. Just as I seized the door handle, I noticed that an envelope had been inserted right above it. Had I been more levelheaded, I probably would have disregarded it. I certainly wasn't in the mood for any more of this loony game. Completely frantic, I snatched it without thinking and rushed outside. The bells jingled sharply behind me.

6

I ran across the sidewalk, almost collided with a woman, then stopped on the curb as though at the edge of a cliff. Frozen to the spot, I couldn't look behind me. I felt doubly humiliated. Most of all because I'd succumbed to fear. Of everything they'd filmed so far, this panicked retreat was the most mortifying. If I'd had to playact it, such authenticity would have been impossible. How could I, a person who looks death in the face every day, be afraid of something in the dark, like a child left alone in a room without a light? And then, what must the passersby think of me, seeing me burst out of a closed secondhand bookstore? Luckily, I hadn't taken anything with me and didn't continue to run, so I probably didn't look like a burglar. Maybe just somebody who's slightly nuts, which would be nothing new. I'd made my peace with being considered that long ago.

Finally, when I felt that enough time had passed, I slowly turned around. Nothing unusual seemed to be going on. Passersby were going about their business, paying no attention to me. But that would be just an illusion, of course. One look at the bookstore and I knew they were still there. When I'd run out a moment before I'd neglected to close the door behind me. Actually, I'd left it wide open. Now it was closed. I'd be willing to bet it would be locked, too, if I were to try to go back inside.

Hesitating which way to go, I finally headed left. This choice, of course, had nothing to do with the fact that the lady in purple had gone that way. It made no difference which direction I took. I no longer had the slightest doubt that they would follow me whichever way I went. Even so, there was no sense in playing the fool and staring suspiciously at the people I passed or turning to look behind me all the time. I already had enough experience with them to know that their spying would be subtle and imperceptible. Just as befitted a masterfully prepared hidden camera episode.

Walking slowly along the row of secondhand stores, I started to wonder whether I could still beat them at their own game. My injured pride wouldn't leave me in peace. The simplest thing would be to break it off and go home. This would certainly foil their intentions. But if I hadn't done it before, now it made even less sense. In any case, giving up isn't the best remedy for injured pride. What if I stopped and said loudly and clearly, "Gentlemen, we've had a lovely time but enough is enough, the time has come to find another leading man." But what if they turned a deaf ear? If I were in their shoes, that's just what I'd do. If they were both filming and following me, it would be just the kind of scene they wanted for this type of show. I would look like a madman talking to himself in the middle of the street. No, I didn't dare hope that they'd end the show just because I was no longer willing to take part in it.

So I had no choice. The show would go on regardless of what I wanted, and all I could do was prepare for the next scene as best I could, to avoid being duped once more. Or at least reduce the chances of it. The thought of the new scene reminded me of the envelope I'd grabbed

65

as I rushed out of the bookstore. I stopped at a better-lit shop window full of decorative knickknacks and paper lanterns and opened it. Once again I found something that looked like an invitation. Any thought that there was some sort of pattern to their plan now changed. Unlike the previous two scenes, both the place and the time were different. Instead of being indoors, as it had been so far, the new meeting was scheduled in the open air. Also, I didn't have to rush at breakneck speed anywhere. The zoo wasn't far away and I had a good fifty minutes until nine o'clock.

I crumpled the envelope and invitation and continued down the street. I threw them theatrically into the first litter basket I found, without stopping. I might have kept them as a souvenir or even as evidence, but it seemed more expedient to confuse my hidden observers a little. Let them conclude from this gesture that I was abandoning the whole thing. Since they couldn't peer inside my head, they didn't know that I'd still appear in front of the zoo at the appointed time. I wanted to see what kind of plan they'd cook up to induce me to keep playing the game if I decided to leave. I didn't think they'd take it lightly if I pulled out. They'd invested too much in this to let it go so easily. I felt relieved. Like me, they had no choice. We were inseparable from each other.

If I hadn't intended to dupe them, I could have spent the next half hour window-shopping on Chestnut Street. I wouldn't actually go inside the shops. After what had just happened, I preferred to be outside among the crowd, something I usually don't enjoy. If I stayed in this neighborhood, however, it would be clear to them that I was just bluffing. No, I had to go somewhere. But where? The most convincing thing would be to head home. I wouldn't have time to get there and back on the tram, but I could go part way, then get off at a stop in the middle and take the opposite tram back until I got close to the zoo. Although the idea seemed good, it had one drawback. The first thing they would expect would be for me to go back to my apartment. If they wanted to prevent me from backing out, some sort of obstacle must be lying in wait there.

I had to choose another direction, one they would never suspect. Although they were extremely well organized, they still couldn't foresee every possibility. Particularly not those that were haphazard and not calculated. I would head in a direction I had no reason to take. I could do it on foot, but it would be better if I took public transportation. I noticed that buses were going along the street. There had to be a bus stop close by. I'd find it and get on the first bus that appeared. The direction it took made no difference. I would act just as if I'd taken the tram home. I would ride for a quarter of an hour and then come back. I would have just enough time to walk from here to the zoo. The thought of the confusion I'd cause when I disappeared from sight caused me to smile.

I came across a bus stop about a hundred meters later. Three people were waiting there. Two elderly women were standing at one end under the mushroom-shaped shelter, talking softly, and a young man was at the other end, leaning against a metal pole, deeply engrossed in his music. A wire traveled from small earphones to a

Walkman in the inside pocket of his denim jacket. I joined them, standing somewhat aside. No one paid any attention to me. At least that's how it appeared. But I had to be careful. Looks can be deceiving and I was under close and crafty supervision. The only thing I was sure of was that no one there was in disguise. None of the three enchanting members of the hidden camera team I'd met could be transformed into two old ladies and a young man. What if one of them was a new member who'd been assigned to keep an eye on me? They were pretending not to notice me, but that didn't mean a thing. When I got on the bus they'd get on with me.

This made me change my initial intention. I wouldn't get on the first bus. I'd wait for them to get on. The one who let the bus go like I did would be the one spying on me. I looked up at the sign with the route numbers. Two routes stopped here, so the interval between the buses couldn't be very long. Indeed, a bus on route 83 soon arrived. Three doors opened. A short, stout man got out of the middle one and walked briskly in the direction from which I had come. The driver waited several moments longer and when he was sure that no one wanted to get on, he closed the doors and continued on his way.

Nothing seemed to have changed at the bus stop. The elderly women continued to chat in low voices and the young man's eyes were half closed as he nodded his head in time to a beat that only he could hear. I naturally found him suspicious. Spying requires a mobility that doesn't go with advanced age. People that old shouldn't even take part in this kind of program, it doesn't suit them. But then, I wasn't sure. You can follow someone in a bus sitting down, and two retired actresses would certainly have nothing against a little extra income. Why should a hidden camera episode be worse than doing a commercial that was full of working-age actors?

When a new bus soon arrived, also a number 83, my distrust in the self-evident was substantiated. A young girl with very short, light blonde hair jumped out of the back door and went up to the young man. He took off his earphones. They kissed and then headed down the street with their arms around each other, talking gaily. All right, that cleared up the situation. Now I knew what I had to do. If the next bus was another 83, I'd get on it. The two ladies would have no excuse for getting on with me, since they'd let the previous two buses on that route go by. If they did get on, then I would get out at the last moment just before the door closed, as though I'd accidentally entered the wrong bus. They wouldn't have time to do the same thing, and if they did they wouldn't dare because that would give them away. If the next bus was a 57, then I'd calmly let them get on it. Once again they'd have no excuse to do otherwise. Whoever stood at a bus stop just to talk and not wait for a bus? There was no third route.

A number 57 bus arrived at the stop soon after. No one got out of it. The elderly ladies slowly climbed up the steps to the middle door and sat in two empty seats on the opposite side. I watched them carefully for as long as I could see them while the bus pulled away, but neither turned around even for a second to check what I was doing. Very professional. Just like they were real spies and not actresses. I smiled in satisfaction once again. I'd skillfully gotten rid of my escort. I would get onto the next bus, whichever one it was. I didn't know where either one of these routes went. For my purposes it made no difference anyway.

My satisfaction was of short duration. Just as the bus with the elderly women disappeared down the street, a woman joined me under the mushroom. She stood a bit in front of me, so I could observe her unobtrusively. She was wearing a beret over flowing straight brown hair. She had an unusually long coat with the collar turned up. Under her left arm was a large thin square package, probably a picture, in dark blue wrapping paper, tied with twine. My smiled melted into a sour grimace. I had underestimated them. They'd left nothing to chance. If the first tandem failed, a willing substitute was waiting nearby.

Now what should I do? I could repeat the game I'd just played: force her to get onto one of the two buses if she didn't want to show her hand. But I would waste a good ten minutes in the process, and afterwards what if they sent someone new? My plan would go up in smoke. Instead of going for a half-hour ride somewhere, I'd spend the time here, giving them the chance to film a nice, unplanned episode. You could be detained at a bus stop if you were caught up in conversation with someone, but to let buses go by for no reason, now that was odd. I had to make a move.

I got onto the 83 as soon as the door opened, not waiting to see what the woman with the painting would do. I didn't sit down, even though there were lots of empty seats. Barely five or six passengers were on the bus. I looked out the window towards the other side of the street. It wasn't until we were some distance from the bus stop that I turned around and looked towards the back. The woman had not followed me. This was meant to make me feel relieved, but it didn't. Instead, my head swelled with serious questions. They weighed heavily on me, so I sat down on the closest seat to make the load easier to bear.

Had I let paranoia get the upper hand? When you realize you're the target of a hidden camera show, the worst thing that happens is you can't get rid of your distrust. Regardless of how warranted it is, it can also lead you to completely erroneous conclusions. If I hadn't been under its sway, the incident at the bus stop would have seemed quite different. Normal. A young man waiting for his girlfriend; two elderly women talking as they waited for the bus; a woman who has bought a painting and is now going home. None of them had even turned to look at me, although they should have since I'd given them ample reason. I was the only one who didn't act normally. I scrutinized the people around me, looked them up and down, I let buses go by and in general acted strangely. I was fortunate, actually, that no one had called the police to come and investigate.

The same thing had happened in the secondhand bookstore. I'd spent almost a full hour convinced that they were spying on me and had adjusted my behavior accordingly, and in the end it turned out that the only reason I'd been brought there was for the last five minutes. Instead of concentrating on what had happened in the back room, for that alone was important, here I was driving myself crazy imagining that ordinary people were following me. If I didn't force myself to my senses, it would be easy to see someone working for the hidden camera among these scattered passengers. If they really were, then no amount of caution would help me. There would be no way to defend myself against such a complex and all-encompassing setup. Then again, what television station would find a project worthwhile if it cost considerably more than the expected profit: having a bit of fun at the expense of a harmless citizen? The very fact that they'd been involved with my humble self for several months greatly exceeded a typical hidden camera show's capacity. Anything beyond that was quite incredible and preposterous.

I didn't have to be on this bus, just as there'd been no point in my searching for a book in the bookstore. I hadn't put anyone in a tight spot. They couldn't care less what I did in the meantime, until the next scene. They were convinced that I'd appear in front of the zoo at nine, just as they'd been certain I'd stay at the used bookstore until closing time. Human psychology is rather predictable. The success of these programs is based on that very fact. In any case, even I knew that I'd be there at the appointed hour. So I could have gotten off at the next stop, but I decided to stay on. I couldn't think of any better way to spend the next half hour. I'd do what I'd originally intended, even though I no longer had any reason. I'd stay on the bus for a while and then take a bus back in the opposite direction. It was actually much more comfortable there than if I were outside. There was no crowd, it was warm, I was sitting down and it didn't cost a thing because I have a monthly transport pass. I would be able to think in peace.

I stared out the window. The dark streets changing in rapid succession mixed with the more or less vague reflection of my face. I soon paid no attention to either one. My eyes glazed over when my thoughts changed direction. The stunt with the book had been original. If I hadn't been ready for just about anything, I would have been flabbergasted to see a book with my name on it. Not only had I not written it, but allegedly it came from the future. The predictability and superficiality of hidden camera shows were what prevented me from watching them. This, however, was different. The inventive writers somewhat compensated for the fact that I was an unwilling participant.

My name on the book jacket brought to mind an event I hadn't thought about in a long time. Many years before, when I'd just started working as an undertaker, I'd been briefly enthralled with the idea of writing a book. It was supposed to be a melodrama. I had the subject worked out to the finest detail in my head. It was a very romantic and exciting story. About love and death. A very successful film could have been based on it. But nothing came of it because I got stuck on the title. I couldn't start writing without a proper title. I'd ruminated a full two-and-a-half months, writing pages and pages of possible titles, but not one satisfied me completely. In the end I gave up and burned everything. I wasn't destined to become a writer if I couldn't even think of a title. I went back to cremations and burials without the slightest enthusiasm.

The thinning lights outside indicated that we were slowly reaching the suburbs. The bus window mostly reflected my pensive face against a dark background. I pulled myself together and looked at my watch. Eight-thirty had passed three minutes ago. It was time to go back. I got up quickly and headed for the middle door, grabbing hold of the pole. I pushed the button to signal the driver that I wanted to get out at the next stop. The three other passengers with me in the bus clearly intended to stay on. No one even looked at me. The bus soon stopped and I got off.

I had no idea what part of town I was in, but it wasn't a residential area. An orangish light illuminated the brick façades of square four-story buildings. Judging by the neon signs, they contained various factories, services, or warehouses. Almost none had display windows on the ground floor. I turned around. I was standing alone in the middle of an empty street. It seemed to be several degrees colder than in the city center and the wind was blowing. I raised the collar of my coat and headed for the other side of the street, disregarding the fact that I was jaywalking. Compared to the reckless dash across the boulevard as I rushed to the Film Archives, this violation was harmless. Now there was no one to reprimand me or give me a fine.

The sign at the bus stop showed only one number: 83. I hoped I wouldn't have to wait long. I'd noted that buses were rather frequent on this route. But the minutes dragged by and there was no sign of a bus. Actually, not a single vehicle went by in either direction. The stoplight at the distant intersection went red, yellow, and green at regular intervals, uselessly directing nonexistent traffic. My stifled suspicions started to stir once again. This was strange. A certain amount of activity was to be expected at that time of day even in an industrial zone. It wasn't even nine o'clock. On the other hand, this was a perfect setting for a dramatic hidden camera scene. The victim would be made to think that everyone else had suddenly disappeared without a trace and he was all alone in the world. No, I didn't dare let myself succumb to paranoia again. They had no way of knowing I'd be there. Not even I had known that. Plus, they were expecting me to appear at the zoo very soon.

I turned my left wrist towards a nearby streetlight and glanced at my watch. Nineteen to nine. If a bus didn't come in two or three minutes, I'd likely be late. Now the time crunch wasn't their fault. Now it was all my fault. I could be late, of course, it wouldn't be the end of the world, but I was already too much involved in the whole thing to take it lightly. Being connected means complying with mutual obligations.

At fourteen minutes to nine I had to face the facts. Even if a bus appeared that very moment—and none was anywhere in sight—I was out of luck. With stops along the way, it would need at least a quarter of an hour to reach Chestnut Street, and that wasn't my final destination. Now only a taxi could save me. The thought of a taxi, however, merely increased my anxiety. Of all the means of transportation available, a taxi was last on my list, for good reason. In any case, even if I'd been able to overcome this resistance, there was no trace or sound of anything.

I was already starting to despair when two lights flickered far off down the street, seeming to pop up out of nowhere. After they soundlessly reached the intersection, where they stopped briefly at a red light, I made out a private car behind them. Someone had finally appeared to dispel the ghostly solitude of this place. Unfortunately, there was no taxi sign on its roof, not even one that was turned off. The red light went yellow and then green and the car started to speed up. Just a few moments more and it would rush right by me. I had to act. This was my last chance to arrive on time. I've never had any tolerance for reckless behavior, even under duress. And here I was behaving not only recklessly but suicidally. I ran out almost a third of the way into the street, right in front of the car, and frantically waved both arms.

What happened next looked like a scene from an action movie. There was the sharp squeal of tires on the asphalt, the car swerved and finally stopped about a foot from me. The leading man had escaped death by a hair, to the great relief of the audience. Nothing happened for several moments. A veil of silence settled once again on the orange-colored illumination all around us. I stood there without moving, hands in the air, between two bright headlights. Everything happened so fast there was no time to be afraid. It actually seemed that the whole thing was happening to someone else, not me. Finally, the barely audible noise of the engine stopped, the door opened and the driver got out.

He was a tall, thin man, about my age. He wore glasses and had a thick, cropped beard. His hair had already receded quite high on his forehead but, unlike mine, had not yet started to gray. We scrutinized each other in silence.

"You might have died," he said at last. There was no anger or reproach in his voice. He said it the way one states the simple facts of life.

"I know," I agreed, as though there was nothing else to say.

We both fell silent again. Had someone been watching from the sidelines, the scene would have resembled a surreal heist: a man was pointing an enormous gun in the shape of a car at another man standing in the middle of an empty street, his hands in the air.

Again he was the first to speak. "I suppose you have a good reason for exposing yourself to such danger."

"I have to be at the zoo at nine o'clock." As soon as the words were out, I realized how foolish they sounded. If the fact that I'd rushed in front of his car hadn't been enough for him to realize he was dealing with a madman, this would certainly do the trick. Had I been in his shoes I would have slipped back into the car, driven around this suspicious guy and hurried off.

But he didn't do that. He stood there, looking at me inquisitively. This time the pause lasted a bit longer.

He nodded to the right-hand side of the car. "Get in, I'll take you there."

I didn't move right away. I watched him get into the car and put on his seatbelt. It was only when he looked at me quizzically through the windshield that my petrified body relaxed and I finally put my hands down. I hurried to the other side of the car, opened the door and got in next to him. I reached for the seatbelt to put it on. As I was awkwardly fumbling with it, the man started up the engine and briskly hit the accelerator. The car lunged forward and the force pressed me back in my seat.

Once we were on our way I suddenly realized there was music playing. It was very soft. Had the engine been a bit louder it would have completely drowned it out. I couldn't determine its source. It seemed to be coming from everywhere. The speakers must have been placed both front and back. The right side of the lighted dashboard had a built-in sound system with red and blue lights resembling a small constellation in the dark cosmos of the car's interior. I couldn't understand why the man didn't turn up the sound or turn off the music. This way you could only listen if you strained your ears. I had to make a real effort in order finally to ascertain that it was a composition for piano and flute. A woman's voice appeared from time to time, but the singing was more or less inaudible. And then we started to talk, so this background music faded completely.

"You're in luck," said the driver, not taking his eyes off the road in front of him. "The zoo is on my way, so you'll get there before nine." He hesitated as though uncertain whether to go on, then added, "Luck would have been on your side even if I hadn't managed to brake on time, but in that case, of course, it would have been a blessing in disguise. You would have gone with me straight to the hospital."

"You're going to the hospital?" I asked in confusion. For the first time, my conscience bothered me about what I'd done.

"Yes, but not as a patient, if that's what you're thinking. I work there. I'm an obstetrician. The night shift starts at nine-thirty."

"Oh, I see." My conscience felt a bit better.

We drove along in silence, except for the barely audible music. Although somewhat appeased, my conscience still troubled me. I had to make my excuses to this man. That was the least I could do. He hadn't been angry at my wild exploit and had even kindly offered to take me with him. I've never been good at finding the right words in awkward situations. That's why I'm mostly considered a cold and abrasive person, although this isn't true at all. As I was figuring out what to say, the obstetrician beat me to it.

"I didn't know the zoo was open at night."

"It isn't."

The driver briefly turned his head towards me. "Then you work there?"

"No, no. I'm an undertaker."

I bit my tongue. Once again it had got the better of my common sense. Whenever possible, I don't reveal the line of work I'm in. Not because I'm embarrassed, of course. It is an honorable and responsible profession. Isn't the best confirmation of its importance the fact that of all public services only we are not allowed to strike? And with good reason. Society could somehow manage to survive without any other service, but if we were to stop working for even one day, everything would fall apart. No one would know what to do with the deceased, and they would only multiply. Few people realize how many deaths there are every day in just one large city such as this.

To be fair, they don't deny our importance, but no one is pleased to make the acquaintance of an undertaker. They get fidgety and try to leave as soon as they can, although there is no need. It would never cross my mind to talk about my work. Even I can barely wait to think about something else. They probably regard us as a bad omen. You can't really blame them. Even we undertakers do our best not to meet outside of work. I'm not at all superstitious, but whenever I run into a colleague it's almost always a sure sign that trouble is coming my way.

Now it was his turn to say, "Oh, I see."

Mentioning my profession only made my position worse. I couldn't take back what I'd said, unfortunately, but I could and had to offer a good excuse for visiting the zoo at this unseemly hour. Otherwise when we soon parted ways he would leave convinced that he'd met someone with a screw loose. Another person might not care, but I do. I care what people think about me, even total strangers. I couldn't tell him the truth, of course. If the story about a hidden camera were to be added to this already messy situation, the man might easily stop the car and order me to get out. Or, even worse, he might take me straight to the hospital and put me in the psychiatric ward. Luckily, I had no trouble thinking up a plausible excuse.

"Actually, I'm not going to the zoo. I have an important meeting scheduled in front of the entrance." The obstetrician might doubt this if there was no one waiting in front of the zoo, but I would stay at the entrance and pretend to be waiting impatiently. He certainly wouldn't hang around to see whom I was meeting.

He didn't seem to hear my explanation. He stared straight ahead, concentrating on his driving. I thought his lips were turned up in a gentle smile, but this might have been an illusion caused by the feeble light. We were already in the central part of town. Although still sporadic, the traffic seemed quite lively after the total emptiness of the suburban street.

"We're actually colleagues of sorts," he said suddenly, after I'd already resigned myself to the fact that he didn't feel like talking to an undertaker and the rest of the trip would pass in silence.

"Colleagues?" I repeated, bewildered.

"Yes, as strange as it may seem. Both our jobs are basically concerned with the same phenomenon. The spot where life and death touch each other."

I expected him to say something else, but he kept on driving as though what he'd just said needed no further explanation.

"I'm afraid I don't understand," I replied after a brief hesitation. "Does that mean there are a lot of deaths during childbirth?"

The obstetrician shook his head. "No, not at all. Almost none. In the past childbirth was quite risky for both mother and child, but that stopped long ago. For example, in my long years of practice I've only lost two patients, and they were very special cases."

"So where does death appear in your work?"

The driver didn't reply at once. We were at a stop-light. A group of happy, noisy young people passed in front of us. A willowy girl with long hair turned towards us and waved.

"Death is what precedes the beginning of life, isn't it?" he said after we started moving again. "During birth you go from death to life. During death, which is your domain, you go in the opposite direction."

"I didn't know it could be looked at that way."

"Quite simplified, of course. There are two basic states, right? Life and death. If you're not alive then you're dead. And vice versa. Those who aren't yet born are just as dead as those who have died."

"But those two states of death are not the same," I said defiantly. "I mean, death that follows life is final, there is nothing after it, while the one that precedes life is . . ." I stopped, unable to find the right word.

"Transitory?" he suggested.

"Yes, transitory," I agreed.

"The question is whether that is the only difference between the two states of death."

I looked at him inquisitively. "What else could there be? Death is death, regardless of whether it is before or after life. Nonexistence, nothingness. There's no differ-ence."

"Do you think so?" answered the obstetrician. His voice was very low, so I barely heard him.

I fixed my eyes on him, waiting, but once again he failed to elaborate, so I could only guess at what he wanted to say. In one respect, there was indeed a strong affinity between a doctor and an undertaker.

Doctors might have even fewer illusions than we do about death. For them it is simply the final clinical state. But clearly there must be exceptions among doctors, as there are among undertakers. Just as some of my colleagues haven't lost hope that death isn't the end, in spite of what they see every day, there must be doctors who have a hard time accepting what their science tells them so irrefutably. I must have run into one of them. The best thing would be to refrain from any discussion. If he'd gotten some nonsense into his head about life after death, I certainly wouldn't remove it with any rational arguments. In addition, it would be quite ungrateful to argue with someone who was doing you a favor. In the end, there wasn't any time for an argument. Although I couldn't tell where we were in the darkness, judging by the time we'd spent driving we must have been quite close to the place where I'd get out.

Indeed, after turning right at an intersection, the tall iron gate of the zoo appeared before us at the bottom of a broad street. The small square in front of it was well-lit but empty. There was no reason for anyone to be there. Who goes to see wild animals at night? No one, of course, except imprudent participants in a hidden camera show. The obstetrician brought the car up to the gate, then indicated the little digital clock on top of the dashboard.

"Two minutes to nine."

"Here I am, first to arrive, thanks to your kindness. Please don't hold it against me for stopping you the way I did. Circumstances sometimes force a man to . . . rash behavior."

He smiled and nodded his head. "Of course." He stretched out his hand. "Until we meet again."

"Until we meet again," I replied, shaking his hand. As I got out of the car, I thought how inappropriate this farewell had been. The chances of the two of us seeing each other again were quite negligible. I certainly wouldn't be needing his professional services and should he need mine, well, the meeting would be one-sided.

I stood next to the pavement, watching as he turned the car and drove swiftly off. I didn't have to pretend that I was waiting for someone. A few moments later he turned right down a street and disappeared from view. I sighed deeply and then turned towards the wrought iron bars. Only a small area on the other side of the gate was illuminated by a floodlight. Beyond that there was pitch darkness.

7

The moment I looked through the bars, the lights in the zoo flashed on. The network of tall three-armed lampposts extended deep inside, creating an archipelago of round bright islands that parted the sea of darkness. Cubicles of light revealed cages, little houses, lawns, paths, benches, and half-bare treetops. This brought relief; the next scene, whatever it was, would occur in a place where I could see. It wouldn't be much fun moving around among the animals in the dark, even if they were in cages. My delight may have been premature, however. Lights can be turned off just as easily as they can be turned on. In the previous two incidents there had been light at first and then I'd been plunged into total darkness.

I stood there, waiting to see what would happen next. Other people were running this show and my job was to adjust my actions according to theirs. But nothing happened. I assumed they wanted me to go inside. It didn't seem probable that the next scene would take place out here. The inside of the zoo was much more promising as a stage for hidden camera scenes than the empty square in front of the entrance. Would they have turned the lights on otherwise? Before me rose the closed gate, and no one appeared to unlock and open it. They didn't expect me to jump over the ominous spikes at the top, did they? Even had I been willing, I didn't think I could. I've never been the type to do such foolhardy things.

Maybe I didn't have to jump over it. Who was to say the great gate was locked? Before reaching for the large curling handle I looked all around me. The organizers had already shown their great foresight and diligence, but not even they could exclude the possibility of someone happening by who might find my entering the zoo this late at night suspicious, even with the lights on. If the police were informed, it might ruin everything. Luckily there was no one nearby. Far off down the street I could see two small figures walking in the other direction, their backs turned to me.

I had to press very hard to get the handle to move. Then I pushed the gate, but it didn't budge. It wasn't until I used both hands that the hinges squeaked and it finally started to swing away from me. I opened it just enough to squeeze through, then quickly closed it behind me, which also required considerable effort. I immediately regretted it. What if I needed to get out of the zoo as fast as possible? Not that some wild animal would be chasing me—they certainly wouldn't go that far—but there might be some other reason. On the other hand, I couldn't leave the gate ajar. There was no one in front of the zoo just now, but someone might appear and alert the police. Better leave the gate closed. It wasn't locked, that was the main thing.

I stood by the gate for a while, pondering which way to go. The invitation had not given any details, and as far as I could remember from the last time I'd been there many years before, the zoo was quite large. It would take at least an hour and a half to visit everything, stopping briefly at each cage. I hadn't come to look at the animals, so I could move more quickly, but on the other hand I'd be slowed down by the fact that I had no idea why they'd brought me there. A totally unexpected surprise was lying in wait for me somewhere. In truth, what kind of hidden camera show would this be if the victim knew what was in store for him?

The trap didn't seem to be next to the entrance where prying eyes might see. It lay somewhere deep inside, where only the animals would be witnesses. I realized that this fact could have hampered the screenwriters. Nothing spectacular should happen in this scene. The zoo administrators would never let anything disturb their animals. It was surprising enough that they'd allowed this to take place in the zoo, regardless of how benign it was intended to be. The demon of commercialization had clearly sunk its claws in deep, although serious restrictions must be in effect in this case. There would be an outcry from both the SPCA and the general public if these innocent creatures suffered the slightest abuse.

I briefly examined the large rectangular map of the zoo next to the entrance. Without any text, just drawings of animals, the picture resembled a winding labyrinth, or a game board that had been placed upright. Three paths forked in front of me. As noted on the sign at the beginning of the left-hand path, if you wanted to visit the whole zoo that was the one to take. Wide yellow arrows to guide the visitors were drawn in the middle of the asphalt at short intervals. The middle path, with blue arrows, was a shortcut to the cages of the most popular animals. Four round signs resembling traffic symbols were placed in a row with caricatures of an elephant, a lion, a giraffe, and a monkey. The right-hand path was the way out. The yellow and blue arrows alternated on it, pointing towards the gate. At some point the first two paths joined and continued together to the exit.

I chose the left-hand path. Were I to take the middle one I might not go where the new scene was to take place, since it was a shortcut and didn't reach many parts of the zoo. The right-hand path didn't have that drawback. If I followed the yellow signs on it, I'd make the full tour, like the left-hand one, but backwards. I could have taken it, but walking against the arrows would have felt odd. Like trying to go down the up escalator. My propensity for an orderly and systematic approach was best served by going in the right direction.

The first cages were about fifty meters away. The map indicated that birds came first. As I made my way towards them, it occurred to me that I had no idea what wild animals do at night. Do they sleep, as one would naturally expect? I'd wondered about the same thing when I bought the aquarium, then spent a wakeful night in order to see whether the fish would go to sleep. I'd also been curious to know what fish look like when they sleep. Do they close their eyes? Do they sink to the bottom and settle on the sand where it's comfortable? Or maybe they don't sleep? That wouldn't be surprising. The struggle for survival that's behind all their instincts is much harsher than on land. Whoever blinked for a split second would be eaten. This was true even in the apparently tranquil world of the aquarium. By morning, however, I was no wiser than the night before. All

I noticed was that somewhere in the dead of night the fish seemed to swim more sluggishly, but this was just my impression because I was tired. The only use I'd had from the secondhand store's book on tropical fish was its divulgence of the fish's secret about sleeping.

From what I could remember from films about wild animals—which I thoroughly enjoy watching on television, even though the cruelty of that world horrifies me—all land creatures sleep. The cycle of day and night acts on all the inhabitants of the planet's surface with a central nervous system, though this influence is much reduced in the aquatic world. Did that mean that the lights were disturbing the sleep of these animals used to peaceful nights? If so, any expected restlessness couldn't be heard. Actually, as soon as I moved away from the entrance I seemed to enter the kingdom of silence. There was no other sound than the wind in the bare branches of the trees. No rustling, murmuring, or twittering came from the area in front of me, and certainly no roaring, growling, or shrieking. It was as though I'd entered a park that was shunned even by insects.

Maybe the zoo animals had become accustomed to city conditions. The sky in a large city is considerably brighter than where they came from, so perhaps a bit of additional light didn't make much difference. But even if the light hadn't wakened them, it was hard to believe they all slept without making the slightest sound. Some sort of background noise seemed inevitable. Well, I'd find out what was going on soon enough. It wasn't far to the first large cage, and it had a three-armed lamppost in front of it.

I stopped before it and looked inside. According to the sign on the fence, this should be filled with quail, pheasant, partridge, and grouse. But there wasn't a single bird anywhere. The well-lighted interior echoed emptily. I looked at the cage next to it with "cranes" on its sign, but there wasn't a soul inside, nor was there anything in the one next to that, which was too far away to read what it was supposed to contain. I turned to the other side. Instead of a cage there was a tall chain-link fence that bordered the ostrich enclosure. It also was empty, but at the bottom next to the zoo's external wall was a possible answer to this bewildering absence of animals. The door on the little house down there was closed, and it had no windows. As long as it was warm and dry inside, these large birds probably didn't miss the windows much on such a cold autumn night.

There was no shelter, however, for the birds across the way. That could only mean they'd been moved to somewhere else for the night. But where? Taking them out of the zoo would be difficult. The only possibility was that shelters existed underground where the animals went every night to spare them from the low temperatures. I'd never heard of anything like that, but what else could it be? The ostriches were probably in a shelter and not in that little house. Remembering how much work there was just changing the water in the aquarium once a week, I didn't envy the zookeepers who had to relocate this whole menagerie twice a day, morning and evening. I couldn't understand why the inhabitants of the first cage were included in this procedure; such birds are adapted to survive in much harsher conditions and so are many other animals. Not even extreme cold would bother polar bears, for example. There certainly had to be a reason. I don't have a clue about the care of animals. Maybe they hadn't put the polar bears inside.

This nighttime relocation had probably facilitated the hidden camera team's efforts to get permission to shoot in the zoo. There was no danger of disturbing or misusing the animals. It also gave the organizers a free hand. Nothing stood in the way of a new scene. Judging by what I'd experienced with them thus far, I doubted they'd chosen this place at random. Something apropos was in store for me. I continued along the path, trying to figure out what it might be. Wild animals live in the zoo and my only connection with animals of any kind was my fish. The only way they could know about the fish was if they'd tailed me when I bought fish food and other little things for the aquarium. How else? They certainly hadn't been in my apartment. I stopped, my foot halfway through a step. Chills ran up and down my spine. I stood there frozen for several moments, then shook my head resolutely. No, that was impossible. Maybe they could get into my apartment since they'd already managed to reach my front door, but they wouldn't dare. Everything has its limits. That would be a break-in and they'd all end up in jail. What normal person would risk going to jail for the sake of something that was essentially entertainment?

I cautiously continued on my way, walking in the middle of the yellow arrows. All around me were empty cages and enclosures. Signs indicated which animals were there, but only during the day. Now each one of the cages could be hiding any number of traps. I slowly entered a less illuminated part. The lampposts were quite distant from each other, so the spaces between them were partially in the dark. When I reached approximately the middle of that part, the light around me suddenly dimmed. I stopped, convinced this was the beginning of a new scene. But nothing happened. At least not in front of me. Something seemed to have changed behind me, but I couldn't tell what. I turned around slowly and saw what it was. The first lamppost had gone out.

Not by accident, of course. Since the very first letter waiting for me on my front door after work, nothing had been accidental. Barely three-and-a-half hours had passed since then, although it seemed a lot longer. My evenings are quite monotonous and dull, almost uneventful. I wouldn't normally have this much excitement in half a year. Whatever does happen to me is at most unpleasant, but not inexplicable. This, however, was one enigma wrapped inside another. Turning the lights off behind me was just one more unknown in the equation.

The same thing happened when I was between the second and third lampposts: the one behind me went out. Were the lights going off behind me automatically because I was the only visitor, or were they being extinguished to cut off my retreat, obliging me to go forward? I hadn't intended to go back that way, but what if something happened that forced me to? Would I have to retreat in the dark? Or would the light go back on again as soon as I got close to a lamppost?

I went all the way back to the first lamppost but nothing happened. There was no automatic system. My movements were under surveillance and someone was turning off the lights after I had passed them. The reason for this still escaped me, but at least I'd established that even if all the lights went out I wouldn't be in total darkness. Enough light came in from outside the zoo to make out the yellow arrows on the path to guide me. If I'd taken the middle path it would have been much more difficult, because blue doesn't show up very well in the dark.

Heartened by the thought that I wasn't cut off from behind, I started to walk more briskly. The lampposts went off behind me without fail as the ghostly, empty animal habitats rose all around, and nothing loomed up ahead that indicated I was approaching some goal, but none of this bothered me. Had this been my first hidden camera scene, I would most likely be shaking with fear. But I was already a veteran, one might say, so I maintained my calm. Perhaps even too much for my cameramen. Would they do something to rattle me a little? Or were they unconcerned about what I did until the scene began, like in the secondhand bookstore?

I stopped when I got to the polar bear's lair, a wide and deep hole with steep rocky walls. In the middle was a small lake filled with murky water and in a corner not far from me, illuminated by a lamppost, glistened a pile of gnawed bones. The bear was nowhere in sight. On the opposite side gaped an opening in the rock that looked like the entrance to a cave. He might have gone in there to rest, but how could I tell for sure? And then I had an ingenious idea. There was a way. Not exactly simple, but feasible. I'd go down and see for myself. Just like that.

I'd descend the metal ladder to the space—no bigger than an elevator car, enclosed by bars and a chain-link fence—where the zookeeper threw food to the bear. The enormous animal couldn't possibly make it through the small opening, but someone with a slight build such as mine might be able to. In any case, I wouldn't have to go all the way through the opening. All I had to do was pretend I wanted to get into the lair. If the bear was in that artificial cave, the hidden camera crew would come running to stop me from doing anything foolish. They couldn't allow the animal to tear me apart. If he did they'd lose their leading man and be blamed for my death. What a perfect chance to retaliate by laughing at them.

If the crew didn't appear, then the polar bear wasn't there. In that case, I'd strut about the lair, that place where nobody normal would ever venture. It was time I redeemed myself for my cowardly flight from the bookstore's back room. I cared about the impression I was making. This would certainly show I was audacious. The viewers might indeed be told there was no ferocious animal in the vicinity, but this wouldn't detract from my exploit. It wasn't something I was supposed to know. How many people know that zoo animals are moved to underground shelters at night? On the other hand, what if they didn't want me to look brave? Then my entrance into the bear's lair would be cut out of the final version of the show. That really would be malicious and vile. What if I threatened to sue them? I must have some rights. I had to have my say. After all, I wasn't just a puppet on a string.

The ladder was cold and wet. As I went down, I noticed that my hands were smudged with bits of rust. I rubbed my palms together, but it didn't help much. I'd smelled the stench up above, but down below it was formidable. The zookeeper must have had a hard time, particularly with a hungry bear standing right on the other side of the fence. The head-high opening was even smaller than it had appeared from up above. I'd have trouble getting through it. The bars that surrounded it were rusty too. I wouldn't be able to avoid touching them. If I hadn't thrown away the invitation, I would have been able to use it to wipe my hands. The way things were, all I could do was take out a clean white handkerchief and start rubbing. I probably wouldn't be able to use the handkerchief again, but a man has to sacrifice something if he wants to be a hero. In any case, it was better to lose a handkerchief than my coat, although I feared it would have to go to the dry cleaner's the next day. The stain wasn't too conspicuous, thank heavens, but who knew what else awaited me before the end of the hidden camera show? It would be quite embarrassing to appear at a distinguished gathering in a disheveled coat.

Having finished the emergency cleaning, I put the handkerchief in the pocket that had already been stained by mayonnaise. It would do the least damage there. It was no easy climb up to the opening. I could grab hold of the bars at the bottom of the opening, but it was hard to find a foothold. I slipped several times before I finally kept the tips of my shoes in the chain-link fence long enough to make it up there. I shifted the weight to my

95

hands and quickly stuck my head through the opening, but it was too narrow for my shoulders to go through. I had to pull back a little, let go with my right hand and then put my right arm in first. I bent down as far as I could, and once again put my weight on my feet so I could free my left hand.

That's when I had my first stroke of bad luck. My hat wasn't fixed firmly on my head and it slipped off, landing on the pile of bones. I tried to grab it with the hand that was in the opening, but this sudden movement made my already unsteady balance more precarious. I had a terrible time staying up there and my feet flailed briefly in the air before I anchored them in the chain-link fence once again. I uttered something obscene. This happens very rarely and I'm always ashamed afterwards, even though no one hears me. This time, however, I turned bright red at the thought that they might be filming. I'd really look my best, like someone without any manners. This affected me more than the possibility of losing my hat. I couldn't see how to get it unless I pulled myself through the opening, but if the bear were to burst out of the cave I had no chance of retrieving it. If that happened, I certainly wouldn't think twice about presenting my bill to the real culprits. At least I'd get a new hat out of it.

I renewed my efforts to get inside. If I'd had something to stand on, the best thing would be to stick both arms forward, as though about to dive into water. I thought it would be easier for the rest of my body after my arms were inside. As it was, without any support, all I could do was bend my left arm at the elbow and hold it close to my body, and try to pull myself through that way. I had got about halfway through when I realized I couldn't go any further. In this position I was too wide for the opening. There was nothing left to do but go back and try something else. I probably would have done so too if I hadn't had my second stroke of bad luck. I started wriggling backwards, but nothing happened. I didn't budge an inch. I tried with all my might, but only got a flushed face as a result. I grabbed hold of a vertical bar under the opening from the inside, and tried once more. Again nothing happened. As beads of sweat broke out over my forehead, I had to face the fact that I was stuck. As if this weren't enough, everything around me suddenly went black. The lamppost right next to the fence above had gone out.

This did have its upside, of course. Had I managed to wriggle free right then, I would have been gripped by panic again. Nothing would have prevented me from scrambling up the ladder in fear and heading for the exit, taking one path or the other. It would have been quite a scene: the would-be hero running away from the bear's lair in fear. This way, even though I was gripped by panic, it couldn't be seen. My heart was pounding wildly, my throat was dry, I was short of breath, but someone watching from a distance would find me rather composed, like a gentleman in a little trouble patiently contemplating how to get out of it. In actual fact, I was unable to think at all in those first moments.

My presence of mind slowly returned when I realized that nothing else would happen. I was stuck and in the dark, but not threatened by danger. I'd try to extricate myself once again and if that didn't work, I still had one last resort. I'd ask for help from the hidden camera team. That would mean the end of the show, but what else could I do? The episode couldn't possibly continue if I remained stranded there until the zookeepers found me in the morning when they brought the animals back. Maybe we could reach a compromise: they'd get me out of there and we would continue as though nothing had happened. They would know that I knew what was going on, but since I hadn't read the script I would still be able to play the totally unsuspecting victim. There would actually be no difference. I was already doing that, although they didn't know.

My nostrils were the first to inform me that something was happening. The stench surrounding me seemed to get slightly stronger. I ceased all movement and began to listen. All that reached my ears was the gentle rustling of leaves somewhere up above. The position I was in didn't enable me to see the opening in the rock across the way. I twisted as much as my predicament allowed, but this didn't enlarge my field of vision very much. Something seemed to snap behind my back, towards the middle of the habitat, not very far away, but I couldn't be certain. I began feverishly recollecting whatever I'd heard or read here and there about bears, never suspecting it might come in handy one day. I couldn't remember much, but what I did wasn't very encouraging.

In spite of their apparent clumsiness and weight, bears are able to move almost noiselessly. They often steal right up to their prey before it notices them, and then it's too late. Those who survived close encounters with these behemoths had not tried to fight them or escape but had played dead. In this respect, I had no choice. If the bear did approach me, there was no way I could fight him or get away, even if I'd wanted to. Nor could I count on anyone's help. Was there really anybody close by? I'd concluded that I was under surveillance because the lampposts went out after I passed them, but the one above me had gone out without my having passed it. Even if someone was there, who would risk helping me bare-handed?

So, I had to play dead. I greatly doubted that I'd be able to pull it off. It might work until I saw him, but as soon as that colossus got close to me I'd go to pieces and lose all self-control. Then a saving thought came to mind. I would close my eyes. That would make my acting seem real. Corpses don't see, do they? I closed my eyes and waited. My heart started to pound wildly once again, my throat was parched and scratchy, but I kept my mouth firmly shut and breathed through my nose, without making a sound. If this wasn't enough, I soon wouldn't have to pretend I was dead.

Time passed unbearably slowly. Worst of all, I could only figure out indirectly what was happening around me. There was still no noise, but I thought I could feel something's stinking presence right next to me. At one point something moist and snuffling seemed to brush against my forehead. I stopped breathing altogether. I didn't start breathing again until the pressure in my lungs caused stars to swim under my closed eyelids. When this same sensation of being touched was repeated on my left ear, my body suddenly drooped. I wouldn't make it through a third time. But there was no third time. This drooping had done the trick. My stiffened body relaxed just enough that I was no longer stuck in the opening like a cork in a bottle. Slipping out, I sagged to the ground like a bag of cement.

I lay there on the ground without moving, not because I still wanted to play dead but because exhaustion prevented me. I expected the bear to growl angrily when he saw his prey escape after being within claw's reach, to pull at the bars and fence in frustration. But there was none of that. Silence continued to reign. He must have been really confused. He'd never been offered such a mouthful before. I had to take advantage of this and withdraw as inconspicuously as possible. Several long moments passed before I was able to move. My eyes still tightly shut, I felt for the ladder in front of me, got up and started climbing slowly. It took an inordinate amount of will to suppress the urge to scurry like a cat up a tree before a pack of dogs.

I kept my eyes shut until I reached the top. I didn't have the courage to look down. I was afraid that whatever I saw down there would haunt me for a long time to come. It was better not to find out what the beast looked like that had almost devoured me. Ignorance is sometimes bliss. And even if I'd wanted to look down there, it wouldn't have been easy. The darkness around me was deeper than I'd expected. While I'd been suffering in anguish, stuck down there, several more lampposts had gone out in addition to the one above the polar bear habitat. A good hundred meters separated me from the next one that was lit. When I started walking in that direction, it went out too.

This made me quicken my steps, which soon proved to be insufficient, so I started to run, keeping to the yellow arrows in the middle of the path. At first it was a light jog, but when the next lamppost was extinguished, I pulled out all the stops. Running at top speed, paying no attention to what was around me, I still didn't get any closer to a lighted lamppost. As soon as I approached the one that had just gone out, they turned off the next one after it. I felt like the hare striving with all his might, but still unable to overtake the tortoise. Plus, I was rather out of shape, so my breath got shorter and shorter. The zoo was swiftly plunged into darkness all around me, something that should have worried me, but didn't. At least not much. It seemed to be the lesser of two evils. If all the lampposts went out, this frantic running would end. I couldn't keep it up much longer.

I wasn't in total darkness, though. The last lamppost hadn't gone out. It was waiting patiently as I rushed towards it, completely drenched in sweat. Having rounded a bend and come to a straight, short stretch of the path before the only lamppost that was still lit, I suddenly stopped. So this was where the trap had been set. This was where the third hidden camera scene would take place. In the middle of the path, turned towards the cage on the right-hand side, an armchair stood: a large, dark brown leather chesterfield. Leaning against the side facing me was something long and black that I didn't recognize at first. On closer inspection I realized it was an umbrella in a cover.

I stood there several moments without moving. My panting breath and pounding heart slowly eased, but not my overheated state. I was steaming hot. The urge to remove my coat and cool down was overwhelming, but I didn't dare. Even though the wind was gentle, it would blow right through me. With my shirt stuck to my back, I'd catch cold in an instant. What I had to do was the opposite: button my coat up to the top and even raise the collar. It would be quite foolhardy to endanger my health for this madness, and nothing guaranteed the organizers would cover my medical bills. No one had forced me to run, let alone undress afterwards.

I expected something to happen, but the space in front of me was as static as a still life. Was I supposed to do something? What could that be? The choice was limited. I could stay where I was, but what would that achieve? I stood there long enough to realize that it served no purpose. The other possibility was to continue towards the armchair. What about when I reached it? I thought about that briefly. Well, I'd take a seat, what else could I do? That's what armchairs are for, isn't it? Even when you find them on a path in the zoo. If that wasn't any good, I could always get up again. But while the purpose of the armchair was more or less clear, I couldn't figure out what the umbrella was for. It wasn't raining. Well, I suppose all the secrets of this world can't be revealed in a single flash.

I headed for the armchair, watching it carefully as though something might jump out of it at any moment. I stopped when I got near and examined it closely, as if

I'd never seen an armchair before. It was brand-new and still had the fresh smell of fine leather. I started walking around it. There was nothing on the other side as a counterpart to the umbrella. When I came to the front I didn't sit down right away. First I looked at the cage it was facing. It was empty just like all the others, except perhaps for the polar bear's lair. A large sign said that this was where the monkeys spent their days. Wonderful. Now I'd see what was in their quarters during the night. Grabbing hold of the armrests, I slowly sat down. The seat was harder than I expected. The moment my back touched the chair, the three arms of the lamppost went out in unison.

I noticed this without reacting. I'd already become used to the hidden camera screenwriters' curious propensity for darkness. They probably felt the scene would be more intense that way. Like in some horror film. All we needed was blood to make the atmosphere complete. I hoped they wouldn't go that far. I'd have no trouble with a corpse appearing—I'd already become hardened to them—but blood made me nauseous. That's why I don't watch horror movies, even though I know it isn't real blood. Because my stomach doesn't know—it starts turning as soon as I see any kind of red liquid. I've even stopped using ketchup for this reason. But I wouldn't be a horror movie fan regardless of this aversion. It might not be common knowledge, but undertakers primarily favor gentle, sentimental films, which is no wonder if you think about it. We particularly like romantic comedies with happy endings. At one point I'd even wanted to write a melodrama myself.

Something stirred in the invisible interior of the cage in front of me. I couldn't see very much, but something was happening. There was motion that no one tried to hide and the sound of a large object being moved. Then there was silence again. It made me think of the set being changed in between two acts in a play. The darkness lasted a few moments longer and then lights flashed on. They weren't lampposts, but something much stronger. I squinted, unable to determine the origin of the beams that brightly illuminated the monkey cage. Finally, after my pupils had contracted sufficiently, I found their source. Four spotlights had been placed in the upper corners of the cage and were directed towards the central part of the area behind bars. Their brilliance reflected off a large black piano.

In my bewilderment I stared into the cage, although I could take in everything with one glance. There was no opening large enough to bring in that bulky piano. On the right-hand side of the cage was a wire partition that separated it from the cage next to it, and on the left-hand side was a solid brick wall. The same kind of wall was at the back. There was a door, indeed, but it was too small for this purpose. One of the two walls must have had moving parts, or maybe the chain-link fence could be moved. Another possibility was openings in the floor or ceiling that were now closed, but that seemed unlikely. I didn't have any more time to consider this mystery because the door facing me opened. A young woman and an older man stepped onto the stage behind the bars.

Their formal clothes deceived me, but not for long. The girl who had played the usherette in the first scene and the salesgirl in the second was now wearing a long gray dress with a black belt. The low neckline revealed a large medallion that glittered in the bright light. She was holding a flute that seemed to be made of molten silver. She was wearing glasses again, this time with a fancy frame that went with her new look, and her hair was even longer than in the bookstore, although once again dark as it had been in the Film Archives. The doorman, or rather taxi driver, had undergone an even greater transformation. His tuxedo and white bow tie gave him the convincing look of a pianist, but it was his general comportment that clinched it. He looked as though he'd spent his whole life giving performances on concert podiums. He was without doubt a first-rate actor, capable of a wide range of roles. I'd never seen him in a play, but that was because I rarely went to the theater.

They walked around the piano and stopped in front of it. Standing there briefly as rigid as statues, their faces all aglow, they gazed somewhere behind me, as though a large, packed auditorium was back there. Then they bowed slowly. I hesitated an instant, then clapped heartily, just as I would at a real concert. The sensible part of my consciousness warned me that I wasn't in a music hall but in a zoo, in front of the monkey cage, at night, but the other part, which often prevails, found justification for this. It was just playacting. Fine, but so much effort had clearly been invested in it that it would be quite rude if I didn't lend my support. What more fitting thing could I do? I would have felt even less at ease if I'd just sat there without making any response. In any case, my push-me-pull-you relationship with them obliged me to play along.

The pianist headed for the upholstered bench and the flautist moved a bit to the opposite side. As she waited for her partner to get settled, she glanced at me and gave just a hint of a smile, more with her eyes than with her mouth. I'm not very skillful at deciphering women's coded messages, but this one was clear. My gesture had been rewarded with gratitude. The girl then raised her instrument, brought the mouthpiece to her lips and turned her head towards the piano. The pianist raised his hands above the keyboard and looked at her. They nodded to each other. The concert could begin.

I was afraid the illusion would vanish with the first notes. These were only actors, after all, and not professional musicians. Actors can be found who have a good voice and even play instruments proficiently, but I've never heard of any who are good enough to play at a concert. Maybe these two had rehearsed especially for this scene, but it was hard to deceive my experienced ear. Of all the arts, I certainly know music the best. For years it has helped me calm down and relax when I come home from work every day. Over time I have amassed a large collection of classical works on records and later on CDs. It was only when the music by itself became insufficient, like a sick person taking medicine for such a long time that it no longer has any effect, that I'd brought in the fish as reinforcements, hoping they would help me get through the difficult period until early retirement. If they failed me, I didn't know what other option I had.

The illusion not only continued but grew more compelling, which confused me once again. The music that started to flow through the bars couldn't have been played by amateurs, regardless of how much they'd rehearsed. These were professionals, playing a composition for flute and piano with inspiration and even virtuosity. I was immediately enthralled, so the questions that started to mount inside me were easily repressed. There would be time for those later. Nothing was more important than this enchanting harmony coming from probably the most indecorous of all imaginable places.

I'm proud of my excellent memory for music. It's usually enough for me to hear only a short passage in order to name the work and even the movement. But I couldn't recognize this. This in itself was nothing strange. There are, of course, countless pieces I haven't had the chance to hear. The problem was that I was certain I'd heard this composition before. My memory of it, sadly, was somewhat hazy, as though I'd heard it only once, long ago and under circumstances that weren't conducive to music appreciation. When the voice rang out, however, everything became clear. The recognition was twofold.

First I remembered where I'd heard this composition and why it hadn't been etched more firmly in my memory. It hadn't been long ago. On the contrary. Less than half an hour had passed, but the conditions had been truly unfavorable. Had the music in the car that brought me to the zoo been turned up louder, there would have been no haziness. Particularly since this composition was quite striking, as I was now able to perceive on a second hearing. It was almost impossible not to remember it. This unexpected link between the two events suddenly broke through the dam I'd raised before the torrent of difficult questions that required pressing answers. The beauty of the piece being played before me wasn't enough to prevent the dam from spilling over. But the undeniable awareness of whose voice it must be froze this spillage, like a sudden breath from the Ice Age.

I recognized the voice even though I'd never heard it before. It went perfectly with the face that I'd barely seen. It seemed to come from somewhere up above. I looked for speakers in the upper part of the cage, but couldn't see any. I then peered at the door, expecting her to appear there. When I realized that no one would be stepping through it, I was cut by something very close to physical pain. It was quickly soothed by the sweet sound, flowing like morphine through the veins of someone wounded beyond all hope of recovery.

The soprano was a crystal knife cutting slices of space, a tide of clarity that dispelled the natural turbidity of the world, a heavenly pen that drew the shape of a sphere. Music always brings me rapture, but this time there was something else. I had goose bumps. They were not from the cool air of an autumn evening. I was still warm enough from running not to feel its effect. Indeed, to feel anything. Least of all the first heavy drops of rain.

I became aware of it only after the voice finished its part, leaving the flute and piano to build the roof of the fragile resonant building, as they had set its foundation. It was already a downpour by then, but I paid no attention. I stared at the two musicians as though spellbound. In the shelter of the cage, they countered the mounting drumming of the rain with their sharp crescendo. I jumped out of the armchair and applauded thunderously as the last tones vibrated through the deluge pouring down on me. The two musicians stayed there for a moment without moving, like a frozen shot on the screen, and then the pianist stood up and went over to the flautist. He extended his hand and she took it, then they both bowed deeply. When they stood up, the girl caressed me again with her smile. Then they turned and headed for the back door.

I kept on applauding even when the spotlights went out after the performers had left the stage. This had certainly been done for effect. The lights would go back on when they came out again. Shouldn't they respond in kind to such an enthusiastic audience? Certainly they would play an encore. It was impossible to think of a concert without an encore, particularly one as good as this. Maybe her voice would be heard again. At this thought I clapped even faster, making my palms go numb. But the minutes passed and nothing happened.

Finally, the absurdity of my position sank in. I was applauding wildly in front of an empty monkey cage, in a dark, closed zoo, unprotected from the pouring rain. I lowered my hands to my sides. It was only then that I realized how drenched I was. If only I hadn't lost my hat, then my hair wouldn't be sopping wet and glued to my head, nor would rivulets of rain be winding down my face and neck, reaching deep down below my shirt collar. I felt some of these rivulets go all the way down to my waist, and even lower.

In the mixture of still-unabated excitement and confusion, I didn't think of the umbrella. But when I collapsed back into the armchair, paying no attention to the puddle that had formed in the seat while I was standing, my right hand landed on the handle leaning against the armrest. I took the umbrella, removed the covering and unsnapped the catch. As I opened it without hurry, something inside it fell into my lap. I didn't reach for the envelope, which I could only make out by its whiteness, even at this close distance. I left it there on my wet coat. There would be no harm in that. Even if it got soaking wet I'd still be able to read when and where I was expected to appear for the next scene. The future wasn't my greatest concern right now. The past tormented me much more: everything that had happened during the past few hours. I hunched down as far as I could and lowered the umbrella right over me. Its metal ribs touched the back of my head and the handle reached the seat of the armchair between my legs. The black dome completely blocked my view, but that made no difference in the darkness. Nor did it make any difference that my pants were soaking wet below the knee. They couldn't get any wetter.

The unrelenting gusts of rain on the tiny plastic roof under which I was sheltered completely shattered me. They seemed to dispel any thought before it was even slightly formed. There was an upside though. In this state I was unable to confront the questions that had piled up once again with nothing external to hold them back. And what, for heaven's sake, was the purpose of confronting them? So far, whenever I thought I'd figured something out I'd always been wrong. Since I wasn't about to give up, what else could I do but continue the game without getting involved in its meaning, regardless of where it took me? My only hope was that we were drawing near the end. The hour still wasn't late, but fatigue was creeping up on me. I'd had almost no time to rest since embarking on this adventure. Unless sitting in a contorted position under an umbrella could be considered a breather.

In addition to fatigue, I started to feel cold. The heat from running had dissipated and my wet head and clothes quickly absorbed all my warmth. If I didn't get someplace warm and dry pretty soon, pneumonia was the least I could expect. But how was I going to get out of there? Everything had grown black since the rain started and I couldn't even see the arrows on the path. I had no idea where the exit was and if I headed out blindly to find it in this weather, I'd only get into worse trouble. I could only trust that the program organizers were aware of my predicament. They certainly wouldn't let their leading man come to harm. A sudden chill went through me. I shook all over. What if that was the actual finale we were heading for? What if the death of the protagonist were the culmination of this hidden camera? I'd read that porn films were being made somewhere which ended in murder for a special clientele that is not satisfied with ordinary perversities. Maybe some rich psychopath was behind all this, impatiently waiting to revel in the pangs of my death.

I almost jumped out of the armchair. Panic had no time to spread, however, because the lower part of my field of vision suddenly lit up, forcing me to stop half-way. I spent several moments frozen before I realized what had happened. If the spotlights had been turned on again the light would be much brighter. It could only be the nearby lamppost. I raised the umbrella slowly. When it rose all the way above my head, I was completely unprepared for what I saw. Staring in amazement, although what I beheld was quite natural, I didn't stand up the rest of the way, but slumped back into the wet chair.

A dozen pairs of equally amazed eyes returned my stare from the other side of the bars. Engrossed in gloomy thoughts under the umbrella, I hadn't heard the monkeys enter the cage. The rain had probably muffled the sound too. I also hadn't heard when they changed the set. In place of the piano and chair was now a dry tree with completely bare branches that reached almost to the roof of the cage. The monkeys were everywhere: on the tree, the bars, the ground. They were of different sizes and appearance. And they all had their eyes fixed on me. This silent inspection lasted a dozen seconds, and then I experienced one of the greatest indignities of my life.

I didn't even know that monkeys are able to laugh. It might not have been laughter, but that's certainly what it seemed like to me. Not so much by the sound—like a dog's yapping—but by everything else. Their mouths were stretched wide open, showing yellow teeth and red gums, they flailed their free arms and legs, doubled over and rolled on the ground, nudged each other, scratched their stomachs, pulled their hair. But worst of all, they kept pointing at me, giving rise to new roars of laughter. Unprepared for such a reaction, I just sat there, trying to figure out what it was about me they found so funny. The sight of a pathetic man sitting sopping wet under an umbrella in an armchair in front of the cage would be much more likely to arouse pity than derision. At least by human standards. For some reason, however, the monkeys found it highly entertaining.

And then something happened that exceeded every limit. One of the larger monkeys extended a half peeled banana toward me through the bars. When I realized he was offering it to me, I shook my head in disgust. How could he even think of such a thing? I wasn't the one in a cage here and they weren't the visitors feeding me. Angered by my refusal, the monkey then did something even more presumptuous. He hurled the banana at me. He was a good shot and I wasn't far away: it hit me smack in the middle of my forehead.

This first gave rise to a storm of enthusiasm among his friends, and then the inevitable happened. A multitude of projectiles flew my way from all sides of the cage: fruit, bits of branches, pits, pebbles, leftover food. The arsenal included some unexpected items: coins, a key chain, a small empty can, a plastic whistle, a brightly colored rattle, a paper fan, and even a broken denture. I hadn't the slightest idea where they'd got all this stuff. The monkeys must have brought it from their night quarters. During the concert the cage had been perfectly clean, as befitted such an occasion.

I endured the barrage stoically, even though very few shots missed me. When the monkeys ran out of

113

ammunition, I got up out of the chair, slowly removed the bits that had stuck to me, bowed curtly towards the cage, and headed along the path towards the exit. My dignified behavior seemed to infuriate the pack. As I moved off, an uproar arose behind me. The monkeys' angry shrieking was soon joined by the voices of the other animals, which had evidently been returned to their daily habitats in the meantime. The zoo reverberated with the angry sounds of the wild. Even though I knew I was protected from the animals by bars and other insurmountable obstacles, it wasn't the least bit pleasant. One really doesn't need to see a lion at large to be terrified by its roar.

This frightful noise would have forced me to run again had I been in the dark. Luckily, the lights were back on not only by the monkey cage but throughout the zoo. All the lampposts were lit once again, as I found out when a particularly dreadful roar made me jump and I turned around briefly. I then quickened my steps, unable to get rid of the impression that I was being chased. The path with alternating yellow and blue arrows turned sharply to the left just up ahead of me. I couldn't tell where it went because there was no light in that section. Instead of cages, the path was bordered by tall bushes and it was impossible to see through them.

I stopped when I reached the bend. What I saw made me groan. Things like this only happen to *me*: I was barely thirty meters from the tall gate. I'd been almost at the exit to the zoo the whole time. I would have stumbled upon it even if I'd headed out blindly to look for it in the dark, instead of cowering helplessly in that armchair, my teeth chattering, thinking the worst. By the same token, if I'd chosen the left-hand path instead of the right-hand path after entering this place some three-quarters of an hour earlier, I would have quickly reached the spot where the musical scene was waiting for me. That would have spared me from unnecessarily taking the long way around and running, as well as from the unfortunate attempt to enter the bear's lair, the only time I was truly in danger, through no one's fault but my own.

I might have stayed there longer with knitted brow as I painfully reexamined my unique talent for making the wrong decisions and conclusions, if the sound of the animals behind me hadn't suddenly stopped. The hush didn't last long, however. It was replaced by something far more ominous than the previous noise. Through the thinning rain, seeming to come towards me from all directions, was the sound of movement: cracking branches, rustling leaves, stirring bushes, scratching on the asphalt. I realized at once that this could only mean one thing and rushed towards the exit as quickly as I could.

When I grabbed the large gate handle, I could clearly discern the snorting and gnashing not far behind me. I experienced a moment of pure dread when I thought I wouldn't be able to get the gate open, but it finally began to move. I opened it just enough to slip through, but then when I tried to step out something jerked me back fiercely. Whatever had grabbed hold of me let go as soon as I was inside again, giving me another chance to rush frantically at the gate. The outcome this time was even worse: the strong jerk backwards almost threw me to the ground. I was about to start screaming in fear when I realized with my last ounce of sanity what my opponent was. The umbrella was too wide to make it behind me through the narrow passage, and I was holding firmly onto the handle.

I dropped it as though it was on fire and finally dashed out onto the small square. I didn't keep on running even though all my instincts told me to. That would have been the wrong move, since I had nowhere to hide. My pursuers would catch me in an instant in the wide open space. The only way to save myself was to prevent them from giving chase. Not daring to turn around, with feverish movements I felt for the handle behind me and gave it a strong tug. In all probability I've never been filled with such relief as when I heard the sound of the click.

I didn't turn around until I'd run a dozen steps from the gate. At that distance I couldn't be reached by any jaws, claws or trunks. But there was no monster reaching for me through the bars, furious because its prey had got away at the last moment. There was nothing on the other side of the entrance to the zoo except darkness and silence. The lights were off and the animals didn't utter a sound, just as any unsuspecting passerby would expect.

But I was the only one there. Before me stretched a wide, completely empty street. I stared at it vacantly for some time until the anguish inside me finally calmed down enough to let me think. The first coherent thought that came to me, however, put me back into a state of distress. I quickly searched through my coat in the vain hope that the envelope had stayed stuck to its wet surface. Unfortunately, I'd thoroughly removed all the garbage thrown by the monkeys. Along with it was my only connection to the hidden camera.

8

What was I to do? They were undoubtedly waiting for me somewhere, not suspecting I'd inadvertently lost the instructions about when and where to turn up next. I looked at my watch. I had no way of guessing where they'd planned the next scene, but it seemed certain that I was supposed to be there at ten o'clock. That had been one of the rare rules in the hidden camera scenes so far: every new scene started on the hour. I couldn't get very far in the seventeen minutes available, particularly if I couldn't count on any means of transport. Now not even a helicopter would be of much assistance because I wouldn't be able to tell the pilot where to take me.

There was a way, of course, to find out where the new destination was, but the very thought increased the chill I felt standing bareheaded in the rain once more. The downpour had eased, but I was sopping wet and the temperature had dropped by several degrees in the twenty minutes since the rain had started. Just fifty steps from me, by the cage where I'd sat, was the white envelope. In spite of that, nothing could make me go back inside the zoo. I would think twice about going there even in broad daylight when it was full of visitors. I longed to be on my way so I wouldn't be late for the next scene and because I was cold, but mainly due to the eerie needles that prickled all over my back, even though nothing menacing was behind me.

I had nowhere to go, however. All I could do was stay where I was, freezing cold, and wait in fear. When they didn't see me at ten, they would certainly come searching. They couldn't continue without me, and what more natural place to look for me than right where I was? If I were to set off looking for them in all directions, I wouldn't find them and they wouldn't find me. We would only lose our way. I raised the wet collar of my coat and folded my arms on my chest. There was little more I could do. My only consolation was that the sight of a suspicious-looking, soaking-wet man didn't seem to attract anyone's attention. I hoped it would stay that way for the next twenty minutes.

I hadn't been standing there very long when something happened that was predictable under the circumstances. I'd actually feared it would happen during the concert, which would have been quite unpleasant, or in front of the monkeys, thus giving them a new reason to mock me. I started to sneeze. It wouldn't have been so bad if I had only sneezed once or twice. My sneezes, however, come in a long series. Once I achieved a personal record after catching an awful cold during an unnecessarily long funeral in bad weather: I sneezed over forty times in sequence. I was unable to stop for a full nine and a half minutes. Afterwards my head reverberated for a long time, like a big bell. Fortunately, I was home when the sneezes beset me. I was glad no one was around to witness this current onslaught of sneezing. Hopefully it would pass before they came to get me. I was chilled to the bone, but not even I could sneeze for twenty minutes.

119

Nonetheless, I was still sneezing when they appeared. This was not a new personal record, however. I'd only reached the eleventh sneeze when something happened that made me jump up and back away. What caused this strong reaction was the vivid memory of what I'd just gone through behind the iron gate. But even without that I would have recoiled. It was a perfectly classic hidden camera scene, since I certainly wasn't expecting anything from that direction. It startled me even more than if someone had dropped down directly in front of me with a parachute. This shock did have a favorable outcome, however. I thought it only worked with hiccupping, but I was wrong. The moment the manhole cover started to rise in front of me, my sneezing stopped.

I'd had no idea I was standing right next to a manhole. Who ever notices such things in the street? It looked like a seamless part of the pavement. The only thing that set it apart was a ring of small round openings in the middle that let the water drain. As it opened, the cover arched up towards me so that at first it appeared to be opening all by itself. That impression probably disturbed me most. Finally, when it had reached an angle of almost ninety degrees, someone's hand appeared holding onto the top, followed by a yellow shapeless object. It was only when the head turned towards me that I realized it was a large hooded plastic raincoat. The water running off of it made it glisten.

The hood was pulled down low, so at first I couldn't see the face hidden in its shadow. Then the person emerged from the manhole a bit further and raised a lantern with his free hand. If I hadn't already seen him in three different costumes, I would have had a hard time recognizing the pianist whose music I'd just enjoyed. This way, I wasn't even surprised at his arrival. I would have been more surprised if it had been someone else.

"Please hurry up, we'll be late."

He put the cover on the pavement next to the opening and started back down without waiting for me to move. The lantern-light quickly faded the farther he got from the surface.

Had circumstances been otherwise, his confidence that I would follow him obediently to such an objectionable place as the sewer would undoubtedly have annoyed me. Just as I would have been incensed that we were once again in a rush. As though it were my fault. But I was in no position to split hairs. What else could I do but obey him without a second thought? Was I supposed to stay out there sneezing and freezing in all my pride and stubbornness?

As I stood over the opening to the sewer, I could see the upper part of the metal ladder that plunged into the depths. A murky glow rose from down below. I hesitated only a moment before starting down. The rungs were cold, wet, and dirty, but this no longer bothered me. I was in the same state. I stopped before I got all the way inside and looked around. I was glad no one was there to see me go underground. Entry into the sewer system was undoubtedly forbidden to unauthorized personnel. Mixed with this relief was the fear of what awaited me down there. Maybe I should have felt confident that I was in safe hands, but stories came vividly to mind of an underworld little known to those living on the surface.

I was already all the way into the manhole when I was stopped by a voice from below.

"Please put the cover back in place."

Of course. Someone would notice an open manhole sooner or later, and it might arouse unwanted curiosity. This hidden camera didn't include random passersby. On the contrary, it was quite intimate and witness-free. I had to respect this. The cover was heavier than expected, even though I knew it was made of wrought iron. I had to heave with all my might to drag it to the opening. My guide must have been quite strong to be able to lift it all by himself. I doubted I could do it, which would cause some trouble if I had to get out of there in a hurry.

The cover slid into place with a sharp rattle, and everything around me suddenly went black. The ring of small openings formed a barely visible constellation above my head that became even dimmer when rain started to wash down from the street. There was nowhere to get out of the water's way, but this didn't matter much considering the state I was in. I wouldn't have been any drier even with a plastic raincoat to protect me. Thin streams of water fell onto my bowed head as I quickly descended towards the circle of light many rungs below.

For some reason I'd thought it would be cramped down there and we'd have to go on all fours or even crawl through some sort of narrow pipe half filled with water. This preconception turned out to be wrong. When I reached the bottom of the ladder and quickly moved away from the vertical opening and the unwelcome shower, I found myself in something that resembled a tunnel. Its immensity was visible even by the weak lantern-light. An entire underground train could fit in there easily. All that was needed were rails instead of the wide canal that took up most of the lower part of the tunnel. The two narrow, high embankments were wet with rain trickling down from above. Debris floating on the surface made me conclude that the water flowed from right to left.

"Come on, we don't have much time," said the man, his lantern raised high, interrupting my inquisitive examination. He went to the edge of the embankment and jumped down without a pause, but he didn't disappear from sight. The upper half of his body, swaying slightly, was still visible above the edge of the stone slab.

I lingered by the manhole, watching him in bewilderment, and only snapped out of it when he waved the lantern impatiently, gesturing to me to join him. I made for the middle of the tunnel with reluctance, as though something were about to leap out at me from down below. But nothing unusual awaited me there. The boat was small, a two-seater at most, so it couldn't be seen until you got right next to the canal. A pair of oars was attached to the stern, where my guide was standing. He indicated I was to sit in the front, although this was unnecessary, as there was nowhere else. I hesitated for a moment whether to jump courageously as he had, but decided instead to get in more cautiously. Acrobatics have never been my strong suit. I sat on the stone floor, swung my legs over the edge and began gradually to lower myself, leaning on my hands. This support gave way at one point, forcing me to jump into the boat anyway, rocking it quite a bit. If the man hadn't held me firmly by the arm, I could easily have lost my balance and fallen into the water or even overturned the boat, throwing both of us into the canal.

Once the rocking had subsided, I started to sit down on the diagonal board in the prow of the boat, but my guide stopped me before I was fully seated.

"Please turn to face the front and take the lantern to light our way."

I nodded, took the light he handed to me and carefully started the maneuver of turning around. It wasn't easy in the narrow, unsteady vessel, but I finally managed to sit down facing forward, with my back to the man. I heard him fiddle briefly with the rope that tied the boat to a large iron ring at the top of the canal wall, and then he pushed us off with his right oar. First we went downstream, carried by the current, and then he started to row, changing our direction.

He rowed with quick, strong strokes, but we didn't make much progress, because the current was clearly quite powerful. It occurred to me that we'd make much faster progress if we walked along the embankment. I was just about to suggest we change our mode of transport since we were in a hurry when the answer appeared all by itself. Fifty or so meters from the place where we'd set off, the embankment suddenly ended. Had the light been better, I would have seen this before, but the lantern's beam only illuminated our immediate surroundings. From then on the canal extended right up to the walls of the tunnel, making it possible only to row or swim.

Rowing was faster, of course, and somewhat more comfortable, though I could think of more efficient methods than that. I refrained from asking my guide why he didn't use a small motorboat instead of struggling against the current, as though this were the Lethe, where progress served no purpose. He must have had a reason for using oars and as a matter of fact it was better this way. If the boat had had a motor he might have started driving recklessly as he had in the taxi, and in the underground labyrinth his bizarre predilection would have had even more disastrous consequences than up there on the boulevard.

Behind my back came the rhythmic splashing of oars and the rower's heavy breathing. As the minutes passed, I felt more and more uncomfortable. The man was clearly laboring, while I just sat there like a freeloader, holding the lantern, although it wasn't exactly bright. I couldn't get used to this division into leading part and extra, particularly since my ears were still filled with the enchanting music played by the fingers that were now holding the oars behind me. I felt this was an injustice, even though I wasn't to blame for the casting. Should I offer to take his place for a while? No, it would be quite risky if we tried to change places without stopping, and there wasn't any embankment now. What if I proposed he give me one oar and we rowed together? That wouldn't work either. I'd never rowed before and my lack of skill would probably hinder him instead of helping. And what would we do with the lantern?

How could I compensate a bit for the trouble he was going to because of me? I could think of nothing better than to render him a compliment.

"You played superbly," I said, turning my head a little. "With virtuosity."

My ferryman rowed a few more times before he replied, "Thank you," in a hushed, even tone, as though I'd praised him for something commonplace. "Please keep your voice down," he cautioned.

It was his cold manner that bothered me most. I've never liked people who pretend to take compliments in an offhand manner. It's a sign of arrogance and hypocrisy. But then I realized there might be another explanation for this behavior. Strangely enough, it hadn't occurred to me earlier, from the moment I entered the manhole. If they were filming—as they probably were, because why else would he have quieted me—it would be quite inappropriate for me to stop acting like a man who doesn't understand what's going on. And that's just what I'd done by mentioning his musical skill from the previous scene. Luckily, it was a brief remark that could easily be removed in the editing phase. All right, no more unnecessary comments. I wouldn't strike up a conversation and would only reply to a question. That way I would be least likely to jeopardize the role I'd been assigned.

We soon came across a new stretch of embankment. It was considerably shorter than the previous one, extending barely a dozen meters. Judging by the streaming water falling noisily to the bottom of two manholes on either side of the canal, the rain had intensified once

126

more up above. My guide pulled over to the left-hand side. I thought we'd reached our destination, although there was nothing to single this place out from the rest of the canal. But when I turned around, continuing to hold the lantern in front of me as ordered, I saw that my ferryman didn't intend to get out of the boat. He pulled the oars inside, grabbed the ring on the side wall with both hands to anchor us and sat there without moving. He seemed to be waiting or listening for something. His eyes were focused on the darkness in front of us.

I turned to face forward once again and also stared, my ears pricked. If any noise was coming from that direction it was overpowered by the two waterfalls plummeting from a considerable height. I was suddenly filled with disquiet for the first time since entering the underground. Until then I hadn't felt ill at ease, even though surrounded by something resembling the set for a macabre movie. Not even the actors who perform in such films are truly frightened because they know they're not threatened by any real danger. I felt the same way. This was only a hidden camera episode, after all; everything was under control, nothing bad could happen.

But was that really so? Why had my guide become wary, as though shrinking from something which lurked in the dark tunnel? Maybe he was acting, but what if he wasn't? This place might not be completely safe. It might even be more dangerous than the zoo. I'd been given an escort in this scene, not so I didn't have to row, but to protect me in case of danger. I abruptly froze. The man was expecting an attack from somewhere in front of us. He was looking apprehensively in that direction, so whatever happened I'd be the one to bear the brunt. This seat in the front of the boat that had seemed privileged a moment ago suddenly appeared ill-fated. Should I propose we change places? I'd have a bit of trouble with the rowing, but did it matter? Better that than coming to harm. In any case, what was a stunt man for if not to replace the main actor in risky scenes?

Before I managed to open my mouth, we continued on our way. We backtracked a bit and then rowed against the current once more. I lifted the lantern high from the raised bow where I'd rested it because it was heavy. This did little to increase the illuminated space in front and my right hand soon began to go numb from the effort, even though it was supported by my left, but I held that position nonetheless. If something were really ready to jump out at us from the surrounding darkness it would aim for the light. Instead of being right behind its source, I was thus better situated a bit below it, where I still had some chance of avoiding the first attack.

We navigated almost noiselessly. I no longer heard the rowing through the murky, dirty canal water. The only sound that joined the ever-more-distant racket of the two waterfalls was the squeak of the ropes that fastened the oars to the sides of the boat. My ferryman even seemed to stop breathing, but I didn't turn around to see how he did it. What difference did it make? My attention was completely trained on the darkness into which we steadily plunged. Large and small objects floating on the black, mirror-like surface came periodically into view. They were mostly garbage, but something more unusual appeared from time to time: a bottle with a trail of smoke curling from its opening, a little chest with monkeys painted on its sides, a brown toupee, a length of bunting, half a chess board, a plastic canister with something scratching and rustling inside. At one point the carcass of a large, brightly colored bird passed by us. I thought it was a parrot but I wasn't sure.

We continued this way in tense silence for about ten minutes, and then the uniform blackness before us altered. We reached a place where the canal split into two branches. The embankment in front of the fork was somewhat wider and had a low iron railing. There was no manhole there, but closed metal doors were on either side. The lights above them, covered with metal grating, were turned off. I hoped this was the end of the trip, not only because of the sinking feeling that had accompanied it but because I'd started to shiver and shake. The tunnel was not the least bit warmer than the outside. The absence of wind was little consolation. My wet clothes were getting colder and colder.

My hopes were in vain, however. This time we didn't even pull over. We kept to the middle of the canal and my ferryman slowed his rowing, so we stayed in place without advancing. I turned around and gave him an inquisitive look. He let go of one of the oars and brought his right index finger to his lips. This was unnecessary because I had no intention of saying anything. I nodded. He scrutinized the entrances to both forks as though something were supposed to make him decide which one to take. I looked as well, but didn't notice any difference. The entrances to the two tunnels that met here looked exactly the same, at least to my unskilled eye. But my guide clearly had sharper eyes or ears. The boat soon started moving again and we took the left fork.

We'd barely entered the new tunnel when I regretted his decision. I didn't know what had made him take that fork, but it had one huge drawback compared to the previous one. It leaked copiously from the high ceiling. To all intents and purposes I was out in the rain again. This didn't bother my ferryman because his hood was still pulled down low over his face. I, however, was being rained on by drops that were viscous and sticky and smelled quite bad. I suppressed the thought that somewhere up above a sewer pipe had burst and was now dripping on me.

Seeing the predicament I was in, I expected the ferryman to do something about it. He could have lent me his raincoat if nothing else. Why not? Isn't the leading man always more important than a walk-on or extra? After all, I wasn't being condescending or acting like a pampered star. Disregarding the possible origin of what was falling on me, there was my health to think about. If I didn't dry off and change clothes very soon, I'd certainly catch cold. I might even come down with something serious. When I turned around once again, he didn't pay the slightest attention to my wretched state. He just kept his eyes fixed beyond me, somewhere in the darkness, and rowed steadily.

This was outrageous! What were they thinking? That it was *my* duty to put up with this? That by my agreeing to take part in a hidden camera episode they were allowed to put me through whatever ordeal occurred to them? What kind of audience were they targeting? How perverse did someone have to be to enjoy the agonies I was going through? And my helplessness? Indeed, how could I even raise my voice against the way they were treating me if I was forbidden to open my mouth? Allegedly, if I were even to speak we'd be in some sort of dreadful trouble, and I'd naively swallowed that, hook, line, and sinker. But what if this were just a trick to make me stoically put up with the whims of their twisted sense of humor? Moreover, what danger could threaten us in the sewer system? The worst monsters we could encounter here were rats. And the sound of a human voice was far more likely to scare them than incite them to attack us.

I turned once more towards the ferryman to tell him openly what I thought of the organizers' intrigues, but the expression on his face made me change my mind. He had the clenched jaw of someone who knows that something dreadful is about to happen. The boat inched along, even though the current was slower here. I'd already witnessed his great acting skills, but what if his concern wasn't feigned? Was there something in the darkness that I couldn't sense? I knew almost nothing about the underground world. Should I bide my time and wait for a better moment to have it out with them? In any case, this boat trip couldn't last forever, if for no other reason than the fact that he must surely be tired of rowing upstream.

Very well, I would hold on a bit longer. Several minutes more or less wouldn't be critical. At least no one would be able to blame me for ruining things because I hadn't followed instructions. I wouldn't open my mouth even if a real waterfall of sewage cascaded down on me. This decision was much easier to make than stick to, however. Sometimes we make sounds against our will. If both my hands hadn't been busy holding the lantern, one of them might have been able to lessen the impact of what came next. As it was, the sneeze I was unable to repress echoed acoustically in the hollow tunnel like a violent explosion.

Everything happened very quickly after that. The man shouted something behind me. I started to turn my head to apologize for this blunder, but stopped halfway. A multifaceted screech resounded in the darkness before us, nailing me to the spot in terror as I stared in that direction. The rising sound indicated that whatever was making it was rushing towards us. Goosebumps covered my body. The ferryman rowed briskly, trying to turn the boat around, downstream, but we were out of time. The very next moment we were hit by a full-scale attack.

It seemed to come from everywhere, as though bits of solid darkness had broken off and were screeching as they swooped down on us. We were showered by a swarm of dark, fluttering projectiles. When the first ones brushed against my head, I instinctively waved my arms in front of me to protect myself, but the lantern got in the way. I waved quite at random, endeavoring to defend myself from the mounting attack. Soon my hands collided and the lantern slipped out of my wet fingers. The light flew in a broad arc and fell into the water not far from the left bank. I stared at it in disbelief for the few moments as it lingered on the surface before it sank, leaving us in the pitch blackness.

I had no reason to stand up, but panic filled my every pore. All around me was the whizzing flight of now invisible phantoms. I jumped, hitting out frantically at the pouncing frenzy of attackers. I heard another shout from the ferryman, which I disregarded since it was incomprehensible. And then the inevitable happened. My agitated movements rocked the boat. If there had been the least bit of light, I might have kept my balance. I leaned all the way to the right, but forcefully threw myself backwards and managed to stay on my feet. With no firm foothold, however, I couldn't stop myself. I continued in that direction, grasping at the air in a futile attempt to keep my footing.

I had lost all sense of distance in the obscurity, so it seemed that too much time passed before I finally fell backwards into the water with a violent splash. While still in the air I realized that I was taking the boat with me. The little vessel overturned, throwing out the other passenger. When the water closed over me, I was at first filled with relief. I couldn't hear the dreadful screeching of the unknown monsters and they no longer flew at me from all directions. This consoling thought was quickly dispelled by the realization that I'd saved myself from one danger only to find myself in another, perhaps even worse one.

The canal was easily the last place anyone would want to take a swim. It wasn't even water, but rather a noxious liquid. If I were to swallow even a tiny sip I might contract some contagious disease. Or what if some bloodthirsty creature inhabited this fecal water, lying in wait for its prey? As I sank like a rock, weighed down by these ominous thoughts, the realization of a much greater concern suddenly struck home. Before I was poisoned or something gobbled me up, I would give up the ghost in a highly unpleasant manner: I would drown. I'd never learned how to swim.

I behaved like any drowning man desperate to grab even the proverbial straw. Eyes tightly shut, lips pressed together, I started to feel around for something to hold onto. If the boat had just turned over and not sunk, I might be able to reach it. I'd lost any sense of direction, however, and didn't know where to look for the boat or where to find the surface. And time was running out. My lungs were bursting from the tremendous desire for a bit of air.

Stars had started swimming behind my eyes for the second time that night when something grabbed my coat collar and pulled hard. I reacted instinctively once again. Horror-struck, I resisted, trying to escape the firm grasp, but I was as helpless as a kitten in its mother's mouth. I kept tossing and turning until a voice came from behind me.

"It's all right. Calm down."

Several long moments passed before the simple fact finally got through to my frantic consciousness: if I were still underwater I wouldn't have been able to hear a thing. I stopped resisting. First I took a cautious sniff and when my nostrils weren't filled with dirty liquid, I finally got up the courage to open my mouth and take a deep breath. I gulped the air greedily, as though wanting to compensate for everything I'd missed since falling into the canal. In the meantime, the hold on my collar loosened and a hand grabbed me under the arms, keeping me afloat.

I didn't have to keep my eyes shut anymore, even though I wondered what would be the good of opening them since I wouldn't be able to see so much as the nose on my face. When I raised my eyelids, however, I wasn't surrounded by the dense darkness that I expected. In front of me, at a distance I couldn't judge, was a large shining rectangle that illuminated the inside of the tunnel much better than the sunken lantern. Squinting, I slowly turned to my left and saw the man in the yellow slicker, now holding me under the arms.

"They were bats. Your sneezing frightened them."

I stared at him briefly, not knowing what to reply. Bats. I had almost drowned because of them. Once my eyes were accustomed to the new light, I looked around and realized that my fears had been exaggerated. We were both standing in the middle of the canal and the black water barely reached our waists. All I'd had to do was stand up and I would have been safe. I felt ashamed. What must they think of me? Doubtless that I was a coward, muddled, and panic-stricken. I'd surely given them reason enough for that. More than in all the scenes preceding this one.

"Let's go," said my ferryman gently, taking my arm. "We're here."

I followed him obediently upstream. I had no idea where "here" was. All I could see before me was the shining rectangle that grew slowly in size as we advanced.

We'd taken a dozen steps before I finally recognized it. A metal door in the left-hand wall stood open. An iron ladder rising out of the water led up to it. The light in the room behind it was very bright. Or at least, so it seemed to me after spending such a long time in the gloom and then, briefly, in total darkness.

We had got quite close when the radiance suddenly dimmed. A shape appeared in the doorway, blocking out most of the light. Since the light came from behind, I couldn't tell whether it was a man or a woman. My companion in the water drew me to the ladder. I looked at him inquiringly once we had stopped in front of it and he nodded as a sign that I was to climb up, encouraging me with a smile. I hesitated briefly, then grabbed hold of the metal handrail. My foot searched under the water for the lowest rung. I'd just started to climb when a hand reached down from above. As soon as I took it, I realized it was a woman's, but she was strong enough to pull me up, so I was next to her in no time at all. She moved aside to let me enter, then closed the door behind us with a sharp metallic sound.

9

I stared around the room. It was long, lined completely with white tiles, and a row of florescent lights ran along the high ceiling. There wasn't much furniture. To the left was a rattan suite with large light-blue pillows to sit on, a sofa, two armchairs and a coffee table with a bowl full of fruit and several glossy magazines. A palm tree rose out of an enormous pot in the far corner, next to the sofa, but I couldn't tell whether it was real or artificial. The opposite wall had a door in the middle; to its left was a low cabinet with glass doors, filled with towels and terrycloth bathrobes in the same light blue. The top shelf was covered with lots of little bottles, boxes, tubes, and similar odds and ends usually found in a bathroom. Above it hung a large framed mirror.

Most of the right-hand side was taken up by two enclosed spaces. The one closest to me was smaller and had saloon-like doors. The larger space was screened off by a partition made of opaque glass. The sliding door that reached from floor to ceiling was open and a shower was visible behind it. The room was very warm. The air was saturated with moisture and there were wisps of steam. I was struck by the odor of essential oils and something heavy and musk-like, which I was unable to define.

"Welcome!"

I flinched at the sound of the familiar voice. I'd been so engrossed in the surreal atmosphere of this sparkling white, clean room after the darkness and filth I'd just been in, that I'd completely forgotten the person who had been waiting for me. I turned to the left and froze, my eyes as big as saucers. I knew who had addressed me, but I never would have expected to see her dressed like that. She was wearing a blue one-piece bathing suit and her hair was tucked into a white plastic cap. It was hard to imagine anything more different from the formal attire she'd been wearing in the monkey cage just a little more than half an hour ago, even though it seemed to me that much more time had passed since then.

She smiled at my amazement. "You can get undressed in there," she said, indicating the small changing room. "A hot shower will do you good."

I stood there for several moments without moving. I realized that staring like this at a half-dressed woman was extremely rude, but I simply couldn't take my eyes off her willowy figure. I finally snapped out of it and headed where she'd told me to go. I halted after my very first step, however. I was dripping wet and left thick muddy footprints behind me. I was horrified by this defilement of the spotless whiteness surrounding me.

"Don't worry," said the girl, seeing why I'd stopped. "Everything will be taken care of. But please hurry. You have to be ready in fourteen minutes." By way of encouragement, she took me gently by the arm and led me towards the changing room. After the swinging doors closed behind me, she added, "Just put your things on the bench."

The floor of the room was covered with wooden slats. There was a small bench of the same wood opposite the door and above it on the wall was a board with large brass hooks. A terry cloth robe was hanging on one of them and several towels were piled on the bench. Under the bench was a pair of clogs.

I took off my coat and started to remove my jacket, but suddenly stopped with my right arm halfway out of the sleeve. I turned around and looked over the door. The girl was sitting on the sofa across the way, leafing through a magazine. I felt relieved. I would have been ill at ease had she been standing in front of the changing room as I undressed. I hoped she would continue her concentrated reading. I would soon have to take off my pants and then my naked calves would be visible under the door. I would put on the bathrobe quickly just in case. Luckily, it was rather long and would cover me almost completely when I moved over to the shower next door.

Everything on me was sopping wet and filthy. Plus, it stank terribly, which was no wonder considering what I'd fallen into. Under other circumstances, I would have hesitated greatly before undressing anywhere but in my own home, but now I could barely wait to get out of my clothes. I didn't throw them on the bench in disgust, however, even though that was exactly what I wanted to do. If someone were to come in after I'd gone into the shower, the disorder would give them the wrong impression about me. I folded the clothes as best I could considering the state they were in. When I reached for the robe, I was overcome with uneasiness. I would only get it dirty when I put it on. But this couldn't be avoided. Even if I were all alone in this place, I wouldn't walk around naked.

I was just about to leave the changing room when I realized I hadn't taken everything off. I was still wearing my watch. As I undid the clasp, I noticed that the second-hand wasn't moving. The watch was stopped at 10:22. Of course. It wasn't waterproof. It shouldn't have been in water at all, let alone such dirty water. Everything else could be put in some kind of order, but not this watch. I would have to part with it after almost thirty-five years. A feeling of sorrow swept over me, almost as though I'd lost someone near and dear. What good would it do if they bought me a new one, since it wouldn't be the old one that had almost fused to my wrist? I placed it gently on the bench, as though lowering it into a coffin.

I got into the clogs and quickly walked the several steps to the shower stall next door. Before closing the sliding door behind me, I glanced briefly at the girl. She was engrossed in her reading and paid no attention to me, just as in the bookstore. It was spacious inside the shower and there were the same wooden slats on the floor. Two hooks were stuck on the partition between the two rooms. A new terry cloth robe was hanging on one; clearly I was to put it on after my shower. I put the robe I was wearing on the other hook and eagerly turned on the water.

The hot, stinging stream of needles that poured over me was pure bliss. I closed my eyes and raised my face. The dense jet seemed to wash away not only the dirt and cold but all the difficult moments I'd gone through that strange evening. I stood completely still, feeling the tension and fatigue quickly dissolve and disappear. How strange. Only some ten minutes before water had almost done me in, and now it was the source of infinite joy.

But the joy was of short duration. A sudden thought tore me out of my contentment. I started to turn around the shower feverishly, making a close inspection. I then searched the ceiling and the spaces between the wooden slats on the floor. I didn't notice anything suspicious, but this didn't calm my fears. If they had put a camera somewhere, they'd done it so I couldn't find it. They weren't that perverted, were they? They wouldn't dare show anything filmed in here to the public, but what if this hidden camera program wasn't being made for the public? Maybe some sick perverts were behind this, the type who get together behind closed doors and give way to their aberrant passions, watching scenes like this.

I reached for the robe, but then realized it wouldn't be necessary. The stall quickly filled with steam. I turned the water up full blast. This might arouse the girl's suspicions, but I didn't care. A man has the right to adjust a showerhead however he likes. Soon the steam was as thick as smoke. Regardless of the complexity of their camera, they wouldn't be able to see through that. I couldn't see anything below my chin. I was safe. Once again I gave in to the relaxing, comforting effect of the hot water.

A pleasant numbness slowly came over me. I kept my eyes closed and breathed through my nose, standing in the middle of the strong spray that stung my skin all over. At one moment I thought I was floating. I felt weightless, as though my feet no longer touched the floor. I even thought I'd be able to fall asleep standing under that shower. In this state of stupefaction, when I heard knocking on the opaque glass of the sliding door, it was like being jolted out of sleep by an explosion. Totally confused, I said the first thing that came into my head.

"It's taken!"

"You have three more minutes to dry off and get dressed."

I quickly turned off the shower and started to feel through the steam towards the robes. I grabbed the first one I found and put it on hurriedly. What difference did it make if I chose the wrong one since I would soon be taking it off? First I opened the door just enough to peer out. The girl was sitting on the sofa once again, legs crossed, but now she was looking at me instead of reading. The expression on her face seemed to show impatience. She had exchanged the bathing suit for a long blue flowing dress. The plastic cap was gone and her hair was short again like it had been at the Film Archives.

As I rapidly crossed the short distance between the two rooms, head bowed, I wondered whether a blue change of clothes might be waiting for me in the same shade as the others. Blue has never been my favorite color, but I was in no position to choose. I would have to put on whatever they gave me. Before I went through the swinging doors, I noted that all my muddy traces had been removed. Things had clearly been quite lively while I'd been in the shower. Now there was just a bit of water behind me, but that couldn't be helped. We were rushing off somewhere once again so I hadn't had the time to dry myself properly with the terry cloth robe.

Upon entering the changing room, I would have been less surprised to see a clown costume or an astronaut's spacesuit. I stared in disbelief at my own clothes on the bench, clean and ironed. I couldn't figure out how they'd done it. Modern dry cleaners work very quickly, but to put everything in order in ten minutes or so was truly unbelievable. Even if I could somehow accept this magic with regard to my clothes, it was beyond me how they'd got my shoes completely dry and polished. They had been in such bad shape that I'd thought I'd have to throw them away. Leather dries very slowly. Sometimes after I got caught in a strong downpour I had to leave them next to the radiator for as long as three days.

But the surprises didn't end here. On one of the hooks above the bench was the last thing I thought I'd ever see again: my hat. And it looked brand-new, as though brought there from the hatter's, and not from the polar bear's lair. There was no time to try to solve all these riddles, however. At the end, with luck, I'd have a chance to ask them how they'd done it all. They would have to tell me, they owed me that much at least.

I took off the robe, grabbed a towel from the bench and quickly began to dry myself. Luckily I didn't need a hairdryer. In that case I certainly wouldn't have been ready in the two minutes that were about all I had left. I rubbed my hair briskly and arranged it a bit with my hand. Since it was quite short I didn't even have to comb it. In any case, I would put on my hat. In all probability, I'd never dressed as quickly in my life. The only thing

I didn't put on was my coat, because it made me too warm; I would have started sweating in no time at all. I threw it over my arm and was heading out when I realized I'd left something behind.

The watch no longer worked, but it was still a nice keepsake. I could have put it in my pocket, but it seemed more fitting to put it on my wrist. As I was closing the clasp, the changing room produced its last surprise. The secondhand was moving in little jerks. I shook my wrist, without knowing why. Nothing changed. The watch was working quite normally, showing the time as sixteen minutes to eleven, which could easily have been the right time. My face lit up. I didn't care how they'd managed to fix it. I wouldn't even ask them. All that mattered was that it was working.

"We have to go."

I jumped at the girl's voice. I hadn't heard her approach the changing room. I turned towards her, nodded obediently and went out.

"This way," she said, indicating the door next to the cabinet.

She opened the door. It led to a small room, at most two square meters. After we'd gone inside, I saw that all four walls were completely lined with mirrors. There was no handle on the inside and the door closed automatically. When this happened, we seemed to be inside a huge cube. I was surrounded by our multiple reflections extending into the illusion of infinity. I had to look at the floor so I wouldn't get dizzy.

The girl touched something on one of the walls. Since I was looking down I didn't notice what it was. The cube started moving at the same moment. There was no doubt about it. The sensation was exactly the same as being in an elevator. I raised my eyes at her inquiringly, but she only smiled, as did the multitude of reflections around us. Maybe this really was some kind of elevator. But what her smile didn't explain was the speed.

We charged upwards as though in a rocket during takeoff. All the blood ran down to my lower extremities. I felt the need to hold onto something, but nothing on the bare, glass surfaces could be used as support. All I could do was space my legs a little to increase my stability. The breakneck ascent seemed to have no effect on the other passenger, however. The way she was standing one would never know we were moving at all.

I was consoled by the knowledge that taking an express elevator wouldn't last very long. This speed was intended to help us reach our destination in a jiffy, regardless of how high it was. But the mirrored cabin kept rushing higher and higher. I had no idea where the trip through the sewers had led us, but I did know that the tallest building in town had no more than twenty floors. There was no floor indicator here as in normal elevators, but even without one it was clear that we'd already gone way past that height.

Some ten minutes later I had either to accept the impossible or search for another explanation. If my estimates were anywhere near correct, we could have reached the top of a small mountain. Since this made no sense, all that remained was to conclude that I had once again been the victim of an illusion. Although my senses told me otherwise, we hadn't moved at all. Perhaps they expected I'd inquire about this in a panic, but I chose to deprive them of this pleasure. I didn't always have to look like a naïve fool. I would pretend there was nothing strange about this alleged ascent to the lower stratosphere.

A brief deceleration announced our final stop. My knees were shaking so much I barely kept my balance. Nothing moved for several moments. The girl just stood there, a smile glued to her face. When the door opened, it wasn't on the same side as when we entered. The opposite wall slid to the left. I stared out, but couldn't determine where it was we had arrived. I gave her another quizzical look. She stretched out her right hand, indicating I was to make my exit. I did so, thinking she was letting me go first out of respect. As soon as I left the cube, however, the door slid shut, separating us. I was left alone in an unknown place.

I turned around the room slowly. It was large and round, like a ballroom. There were no windows or doors. Nothing disturbed the smooth, white cylindrical wall. It was lit from somewhere up above, but the source was concealed. At the top of the wall was a lateral conduit that didn't reach all the way to the ceiling. The lights were on the upper part of this conical ring, out of sight. Their reflected glow was soft, giving the polished parquet floor a dull sheen.

I stayed in the same place for some time without moving, unsure of what to do. The only piece of furniture in the room was a revolving chair smack in the middle. I finally headed toward it. What choice did I have? It certainly hadn't been put there without reason, and what else was it for than to sit in? I checked it out a bit before sitting down. It was upholstered in dark blue, there were no armrests, and it looked like a typical office chair. A shaft with a footrest at the end protruded from the seat. At the bottom the chair divided into five legs, like a starfish. The legs were not on rollers, however, but were fastened to the floor, so the chair couldn't move.

I looked in the direction I'd come from but could find no trace of the elevator door. If I wanted to leave, I didn't know how to find the exit. I felt like a mouse trapped in a hatbox. Then again, there would be time enough to worry about that. I sat down and put my feet on the footrest. I laid my coat in my lap and put my hat on top of it. I shifted the seat a bit to the left and right. It moved almost without resistance. I touched a lever underneath it and pressed. The seat dropped some fifteen centimeters. I got up and the seat returned to its previous position all by itself. There was no more time for such child's play, however, because the lights suddenly went out.

For the umpteenth time that night I was in total darkness. I sighed. This was getting boring. One would expect them to show a bit more imagination instead of repeating themselves. Their only special effects seemed to be turning the lights on and off. I didn't know what they expected to achieve with that, but if they thought they'd frighten me again they'd miscalculated. Not the least bit ruffled, I sat there patiently, waiting to see what they'd cooked up for me in this episode. I didn't have long to wait. The lights soon went back on, but they came from the wall itself and not from the hidden units up above.

147

I'd never seen anything like it. The great surface that had been white a moment before was now drenched in a deep purple glow, as though the wall were covered with some unnatural fluorescence. The shade wasn't uniform. There were many layers of purple with admixtures of other colors, mostly blue in the upper parts and green at the bottom. It was as though someone had put up a large, shining mural during the brief period of darkness. What it showed wasn't a picture of anything recognizable. Or at least I was unable to make anything out. Perhaps a devotee of abstract art could perceive some meaning, but I've never been a follower of that artistic genre. To me the pattern looked quite random.

I wondered whether the whole wall had been touched by this change or just the part within my field of vision. When I twisted just a little to see behind me, the slight turn set the seat under me in motion. Although this wasn't what I'd intended, I made almost a full turn. Or maybe it was a full turn. It was hard to verify because I had no reference point on the wall. Nothing stood out in particular. The circular surface seemed to be covered with an unvarying, multicolored, luminous tapestry.

To make sure I hadn't missed anything, I made another turn. This time I did it more briskly, pushing my shoulder into the right of the chair back. I made several turns before I stopped. Now I was certain that the whole wall was painted, but this no longer mattered. Something else had attracted my attention. Just before the seat started to slow down, the pattern surrounding me seemed to be transformed. It might have been my imagination, but I could have sworn that the

148

purple arabesque became clearer, transforming in the blink of an eye from an abstract picture into something recognizable.

This reminded me of those strange pictures that were quite popular several years ago. If you looked at them straight on, all you saw was a riot of colors. But if you blurred your vision in a special way, a previously unseen person or scene would suddenly appear in three dimensions. It had taken me an entire evening to master the art of looking that special way. I'd carefully read the instructions that came with the book of pictures, then strained my eyes in vain for a long time. When I was just about to give up, convinced I'd been the victim of a hoax, I suddenly saw the transformed pictures.

It had been a moment of revelation, like accessing a parallel world. Indeed, what I'd seen was only a zebra grazing in the savanna, but that was not the point. The tremendous excitement made me jump and shout. This, unfortunately, had been the wrong thing to do. As soon as I moved, the window into the other reality closed and I was once again before its meaningless two-dimensional reflection. The following half hour was filled with extreme frustration as I strained to see through the surface of the picture, but I forgot all my pains as soon as the zebra appeared once more.

Now I thought this might be something similar. I spent several minutes sitting still, staring at the wall in front of me. I tried the different tricks I'd learned back then to shift my focal distance beyond the place where my eyes were looking, but all I managed to do was strain my eyes. The purple pattern unremittingly refused to lift its veil. And then it dawned on me that my approach was wrong. When a picture had emerged out of the abstraction a moment before, I had looked at it with normal eyes. The only difference was that I'd been spinning.

This time I braced my feet firmly on the parquet, pushed hard, then quickly put them on the footrest. I twirled so fast I had to hold onto the seat next to my thighs, otherwise the inertia would have flung me out like a slingshot. Since the seat turned quite smoothly, I didn't have the impression I was moving. It actually seemed as though I was motionless, while the great wall turned in front of me faster and faster. The purple layers merged first into stripes and then into a continuous, indeterminate background. And then it happened.

The landscape seemed to explode before me, leaving me breathless. I tightened my grip on the edge of the seat, but not from fear of falling. What had once appeared as a revelation was just a pale shadow compared to this. I was no longer a mere observer standing in front of a window that looked into another reality. Now I seemed to have flown through that window, crossed the boundary that divides worlds, and ended up on the other side. The third dimension extended not only in the sense of depth but also towards me, including me.

I was in the middle of a field. It was almost completely flat and extended all the way to the far horizon. Nothing disturbed its uniformity. There were no hills, forests, rivers, roads, or houses. Just a dense covering of plants, a vast sea of purple flowers on slender green stalks below the blue sky. I watched for several moments, spellbound, before I became aware of the fact that the scene wasn't static as it had been in those illusive pictures. Set in motion by the breeze, waves rippled across the floral carpet, changing its shades in broad strokes. I wasn't surprised when I, too, felt a gentle gust of wind in my face, as though I was truly standing there. Anything else would actually have seemed unnatural.

Then another of my senses was triggered. Fragrances smelt by chance can have the unexpected effect of calling forth deeply buried memories. They are quite vivid, even though decades may stand between us. The scent that now struck me, however, was not connected to the distant past. It took only a moment to realize when and where I'd last smelled that fragrance. It had been just a few hours earlier in the Film Archives. At the time I'd thought it strange that I'd been unable to recognize the floral extract used by the woman sitting in the dark next to me. Now this enigma was solved. I couldn't possibly have recognized it when I'd never seen the flower from which it came.

I wasn't seeing this for the first time, however. Suddenly I was certain of it, although I didn't immediately recall where I'd seen it before. The purple landscape rolled and swayed before me, coaxing out something on the edge of my memory. When it finally materialized, like a flash of lightning, I realized why it had been so hard to place. There hadn't been time for it to be etched in my remembrance. I'd only seen it for an instant before the lights went out in the back room of the secondhand bookstore. The picture on the cover of the book I'd ostensibly written seemed to have been brought here.

That picture had shown something more than just flowers. The lady had stood in the middle of it, her head raised, the hat no longer concealing it. Thrilled at this thought, I behaved as if I really were in the field that appeared to surround me. I started to look around the immense panorama to see if I could find her. She had to be somewhere close by, I clearly sensed that. These agitated movements had an effect on the spinning of the chair. They didn't stop it but they slowed it down a little, just enough for the crystal clear world around me first to tremble, then stiffen, then finally dissolve into a meaningless blur.

The same fury engulfed me as I'd felt when the zebra disappeared. Luckily, it was much easier to bring back what I'd lost here. All I had to do was spin the chair again. I took my feet off the footrest, but before I touched the parquet to push off once more, the chair started turning all by itself. I froze in bewilderment, leaving my feet to hang just above the floor. As the spinning increased with no effort on my part, I bemoaned the lack of any armrests. A seat belt would have been ideal. Since they'd taken such pains to set up this complicated episode, why hadn't they thought of a detail like that? The hidden camera organizers' concern for the participant's safety had already been shown wanting on several occasions. I was extremely lucky to still have a head on my shoulders.

Any fear that I wouldn't be able to stay on the chair disappeared as soon as the purple sea swelled around me once again. In this world there was no reckless spinning, no threat of danger. Here everything exuded peace, tranquility, and calm. This was probably how the faithful imagined paradise, the Elysian fields. Just as this crossed my mind, however, something disturbed the unchanging idyll. Something was emerging from the floral carpet, approximately halfway toward the horizon. It was as though someone had been lying there unnoticed and was now getting up from the flowers. The clothes the person was wearing were of the same hue and blended into the surroundings. The figure was standing too far away to tell who it was, but proximity wasn't necessary. I realized at once who it had to be.

I watched as she drew closer. She left only a brief wake behind her since the flowers bounced back at once on their supple stalks. The purple-crowned blades reached her knees and she touched them with her fingertips. She seemed to be gliding, not walking. She was moving straight ahead, the broad hat brim lowered almost to her chest. In such a position, it wasn't clear to me how she managed to head straight in my direction. She seemed to be going along some invisible path. Or maybe I was in some sort of center and all the paths led to it.

I didn't know what would happen when she came right up to me. I was suddenly filled with anxiety. I had a burning desire to see her at last—which was why I'd put up with all the nuisance and abuse—but it would be better if we didn't meet face to face. Maybe this wouldn't be such an encounter. This was only some sort of projection, after all. I would see her but she wouldn't see me. Did I dare rely on that? What if only this landscape were an illusion and she was real? That was quite possible. All kinds of special effects are created these days. It might look to me like she was walking through flowers, but she was actually walking from the wall of the large room towards the chair where I was sitting.

The palms of my hands clinging to the seat started to sweat. I might even have fidgeted had I not been sitting so rigidly. My mouth went dry and a lump formed in my throat. My breath came short and fast, while my heart beat like a tin drum. Something strange crossed my mind just then. None of these symptoms ever appeared when they were most fitting, while I was at work. I prepared the dead and buried them with complete composure, without getting upset, with excessive impassivity. These symptoms appeared only on the eve of an awkward encounter.

A mere few steps separated us. I became totally confused. What should I do? How should I behave? I would have to say something to her when she looked at me. Simple good manners required this. I couldn't just stare at her without speaking. But what should I say? What does one say in such circumstances? We hadn't even been formally introduced. Of course, we weren't exactly strangers. Was this the climax of the hidden camera? My complete inability to say or do anything at all when I finally found myself in front of her?

She stopped directly before me. She stood there several moments without moving, head bowed, and then the hat brim slowly started to rise. The tip of her chin had already appeared under the brim when I suddenly realized what I had to do. A gentleman never sits while a lady is standing before him. That would be highly impolite. I would look totally uncultured, and I could by no means allow that. I stood up without hesitation.

154

Better said, I tried to stand up. Nothing simpler, one might say. How many times in my life had I made that commonplace movement? Yes, but never before from a chair that was spinning like a top, while my feet were hanging somewhere between the footrest and the floor. I realized the fatal mistake a split second too late. Although what ensued had to happen very fast, it seemed to take place in dreamy slow motion.

When I flew off the seat, without letting go of my coat and hat, the field of flowers dissolved. It turned into a sequence of disconnected spots that seemed to hesitate a moment about staying together, and then disappeared. They took her along with them, and this removed at least one uncertainty. She hadn't been in this place physically but was part of the illusion. A wave of bitterness swept over me. If I'd waited just a little longer, I would finally have seen her. But there was no one to blame. That's what happens when a man hastens to show his good manners.

I flew for a long time. I didn't even try to figure out to which side I'd been thrown. In any case this made no difference in the round room. As the wall got closer, the purple arabesque on it gave way to a uniform whiteness. I seemed to be falling into it from above, as though into a swimming pool full of milk. But there was no splash. If it had been milk, it was as solid as granite. Had I known how to dive I might have automatically stretched out my arms. As it was, when I went in headfirst, the world around me instantly became its opposite. White became deepest black and with it, quite naturally, rose the silence of the grave.

10

Silence still reigned when the darkness began to flicker, growing stronger and weaker in waves, like a black lid being raised and lowered over me. I could make no sense of the image that briefly replaced the gloom each time the lid was lifted. Something large was standing directly before me, but I couldn't see it properly. I seemed to need reading glasses, except that I've never worn glasses. I haven't needed them. I was proud of my vision; it was still good despite my age.

As the illuminated intervals grew longer, the picture slowly came into focus. Before I finally realized what I was looking at, I figured out what kind of lid was being raised and lowered over me. It wasn't big at all, as I'd first thought, and there were actually two of them, not one. My eyelids were moving, veiling and unveiling the world. I wanted to put a stop to this blinking, but my conscious will had no effect on it. When it finally ended, it seemed to do so if its own accord.

It wasn't easy to recognize what was in front of me even after my vision sharpened. Indeed, the objects were quite ordinary, but I'd never seen them from this angle. The napkin, knife and plate seemed to be standing upright, stuck onto a vertical white cloth against which my right cheek was pressed. The only object lying horizontally was a large wine glass. Had it not been empty, it wouldn't have been able to retain any liquid.

I stared fixedly at this impossible sight for quite some time, trying to decipher it. When I finally realized what had happened, I was filled with pride. I imagined that no less ingenuity had been required to renounce the obvious and recognize that the Earth revolves around the Sun, and not vice versa. This too was a complete change in perspective. The objects in my field of vision were in their normal position. What was abnormal was the position of my head. Instead of my holding it upright, for some reason it was lying on the white tablecloth.

Pride instantly turned into humiliation. I didn't know what had made me put my head on the table, but it was indecorous to say the least. Such behavior suited drunks passing out in pubs on the edge of town, not a man of dignity. I had to sit up at once. I did so, but too abruptly. Suddenly I seemed to be in a little boat in the middle of a storm. Everything around me started to rock, so I put my head back down on the tablecloth.

I put a hand to my head to help the rocking subside. It soon stopped, but a new problem arose. My hair was wet and sticky. I first thought it was blood, but when I brought my fingers before my eyes there was no trace of anything red. There was an unpleasant smell coming from my palm, however, so I moved my hand away. It reminded me of something medicinal, but I couldn't make out what it was. That kind of smell was primarily what kept me away from hospitals or outpatient clinics. They filled me with nausea. Indeed, the chemicals used in my profession didn't smell any better, on the contrary, but for some strange reason they didn't bother me. Probably because I'd gotten used to them.

Although offensive, the smell had one good side. My mind cleared instantly as if someone had put a bottle of smelling salts under my nose. I still had no idea what table I was lying on, but at least my memory returned. I touched my head again gingerly. There had to be a bump there, if nothing else. I'd flown out of the revolving chair so violently that it was a miracle I hadn't cracked my skull when I hit the wall. But except for the thick, color-less, strong-smelling ointment that had been wiped on my hair, there was nothing else. Not even mild discom-fort. I pressed my head all over with my fingertips, but it didn't hurt anywhere.

This was reassuring, of course, although it still made me furious. True enough, no one had forced me to get up off the madly spinning chair, but this did nothing to diminish the responsibility of the hidden camera orga-nizers. They should have anticipated this possibility and provided better protection. People don't always take their own safety into consideration. Even carriage doors in trains can only be opened after the train has stopped at a station. Many people had been injured by heedlessly getting off moving trains; the damages the railroad com-pany had been forced to pay convinced them to intro-duce secured doors. Maybe I could get some damages too. My life had been in genuine danger. Yes, but how could I prove it? Those who'd jumped off of a train had broken something at least, but I didn't have a scratch on me. In addition, I would have been hard put if they'd asked me to show them where the accident had taken place. I would never be able to find my way all alone through that dark tunnel to the circular room. Actually,

I had no desire to find it, regardless of any damages I might receive. I'd had my fill of the underground, once and for all.

The thought of the room with the living frescoes made me face the question: Where was I now? Was I still in it? As far as I remembered, no table had been set there, but that didn't mean a thing. While I'd been unconscious they could have brought it in. On the other hand, in such a state they could have taken me somewhere else. Actually, that would have suited them perfectly, if they'd planned a new episode in a place where I wouldn't have been very willing to go. They would simply present me with a *fait accompli*. But where would I hesitate to go after everything I'd already gone through? I thought this over briefly, but nothing particularly dangerous or terrible crossed my mind. There was no need to make wild guesses, however. All I had to do was look around.

This time I raised my head slowly. The rocking was still there, but it was bearable. It stopped when I sat up straight. I was no longer in the round room. Although the lighting was scanty, I had no trouble realizing where I was at first sight. They were right to doubt that I'd be ready to come here of my own free will. Not because I'd be deterred by religious scruples. There are very few believers in my line of work. This is unavoidable. Nevertheless, there are considerations that must be respected even if you're an atheist; if for no other reason than out of regard for those who do believe. It was simply barbarous to set a hidden camera episode in a church.

This couldn't have been done without the clergy's approval. Mind you, I have no illusions whatsoever about those people. After all the years of working together with them I've gotten to know both their good and bad sides, but this was too much. Allowing a holy place to be profanely abused in such a way was the height of blasphemy. All right, I understand that churches need money—who doesn't?—but there must be a limit. It seems, unfortunately, that everything has its price. I was really curious as to how much this had cost. How much does it cost to rent a church for the purpose of entertainment outside of its working hours?

Perhaps my accusations were unfounded? What if they hadn't asked for permission but had sneaked me in? That wouldn't have surprised me in the least. It's a well-known fact that nothing is sacred to television people. All they care about is their viewer ratings. The more outrageous and scandalous, the larger the audience. And the greater the number of viewers, the greater the advertising revenue. If the church were to sue them for this invasion, they'd have no trouble paying any settlement out of such earnings. Yes, but what about me? If they accused me of complicity, which was by no means out of the question, how could I defend myself? Who would believe that I was participating in all this against my will? No one, of course. That line of argument might work if this were the first episode and not the umpteenth one already. I would have to hire a lawyer, but where would I get the money? Lawyers are diabolically expensive and I had no collateral to help me.

No, I'd be better off if I tried to reach an understanding with the clergyman in charge of the church. They all have skeletons in their closets. I'm in the best position to know that. They might say I was blackmailing them. So what? That sort of thing would be out of place if I were dealing with the immaculately righteous, but since I wasn't, we would find a common language. With some of them it should even be quite easy. I examined the inside of the church a bit more closely to find out which clergyman it belonged to. I am perfectly familiar with all the churches in town since my work takes me to them every day. And then I became aware of something that I should have noticed at once. It must have slipped me by because I was still a little dazed. I had never been in this church before.

An inexperienced person would most likely not have noticed it, particularly not in the prevailing gloom. Churches all resemble each other inside. Especially the old ones, and most of them are old. They seem to be created out of the same mold. But when you spend lots of time in them, and the service being held doesn't interest you very much because you've already heard it countless times, then you amuse yourself by taking mental notes. At least that's what I do. It soon became clear to me that the details of the churches are quite different. I finally became so skilled that I thought I would be able to identify a church by looking at a picture of any of its sections. Idleness sometimes turns a man into an expert.

Now for the first time this expertise was serving some purpose. Numerous details brought me to the unfailing conclusion that I'd never previously been inside this church. But how was that possible? The obvious first thought occurred to me: they'd taken me to another town with a large church. This, however, would have taken some time. In that case I must have been unconscious for quite a long spell. What time was it, anyway? I pushed up the left sleeve of my jacket. Eleven sixteen. If this was right, then not even a helicopter could have brought us to the closest town. Which was good because I was terrified of flying.

And then I felt like slapping my forehead. Of course! What had seemed obvious was, in fact, needlessly complex and expensive. There was a much simpler and less costly way to go about it. I wasn't in a church at all. Why would they pay for an expensive rental or run the risk of trouble with the church fathers, when it could be done the typical filmmaking way? This was just a stage set in a large studio. They'd probably used what was on hand from previous filming instead of building the whole set just for this episode. If I went to the movies more often I might even have remembered the film where I'd seen this church before.

There was something unusual about it, however. I doubted that scenes filmed here earlier contained all that now lay before me. The formally laid table didn't fit at all with the church environment. Even for a film parody it stood on the margin of acceptability. If it had at least had normal proportions . . . but it didn't. On the contrary, I'd never seen a table nearly as long. The end where I sat was right next to the door of the alleged church, while the other end was by the altar. I couldn't tell whether it was one single table or a string of smaller tables joined together, because it was completely covered by a white cloth reaching all the way to the stone floor.

Before me was the cutlery that I'd first seen from an unusual angle after coming round. It appeared rather expensive, but was probably just imitation. Film studios don't have much that isn't imitation. The fork and knife seemed to be of heavy silver. If I didn't know where I was, I would have sworn that the dinner plate was made of the finest china. By the same token, the way the candlelight sparkled on the wine glass made it seem to be crystal, with a gold rim. The only thing beyond suspicion was the napkin placed stiffly upright in the middle of the plate. It certainly wasn't imitation silk.

The same place setting was laid at the other end of the table. The distance made it look very small. Candlesticks were placed between us at regular intervals of about a meter and a half. I counted thirteen of them. Each had five branches. The four outer ones formed a square while the fifth was at the intersection of their diagonals. The candles in the holders were of the same height. It seemed they had recently been lit for the first time, because there was no wax dripping down any of them. The only other illumination came from torches placed high on the walls and pillars. Their flames flickered gently in the smoke.

Did the other place laid at the far end from me mean that I would soon have company? If that happened, we would be in an awkward situation. It would be difficult to talk, for example, except by shouting to each other, which wasn't very polite table manners. In actual fact, at such a distance and with such lighting I wouldn't even be able to get a good look at whomever was sitting at the other end. I doubted this arrangement had been made without some reason, but I didn't try to guess what that might be. All my previous attempts at divining the intentions of the hidden camera scriptwriters had been unsuccessful. The best thing would be to wait patiently and see what new episode they had prepared. Something would certainly start happening soon.

At almost the same moment there came the sound of footsteps to my left. They echoed hollowly in the large empty studio transformed into a church. I turned in that direction and saw a man approaching in the gloom. The last time I'd seen him he had been wearing a raincoat and was waist-deep in dirty canal water. Now his appearance was the exact opposite. He was wearing a dark green jacket with shiny lapels and a large bow tie of the same color, set against a white shirt. His black pants had a crease down the middle and his shoes were brightly polished. The cotton gloves he wore were sparkling white.

Under his arm was a large leather folder of the same green. He came up to me, smiled and bowed curtly. Not knowing what else to do, I returned the bow. He handed me the folder and took one step back. I took it and briefly inspected the outside. On the front was a gold-embossed ballerina. She stood on her points, her arms raised above her head. She was wearing a leotard and very short tutu. There was no inscription.

I had no idea what might be inside. Before opening it, I glanced up at the man. He was still smiling. His arms were at his sides, his hands folded. Inside the folder was another one, somewhat smaller, made of beige cardboard. The same drawing of the ballerina was on the front. There was no text there either. I looked at the

164

man next to me again. His demeanor hadn't changed in the slightest. All that remained was to open this second folder.

It contained a sheet of thick white paper. Something was written in tiny letters approximately in the middle. I had to turn the folder towards the closest candlestick and lean over it a bit. Then I was able to read the text but that didn't help me very much. It was in a language I didn't know. I stared at the short line of words for some time, not knowing what to do. It had clearly been expected that I would understand the writing. I would thus disgrace myself when my ignorance was revealed. I couldn't let that happen.

I closed the folder and returned it to the man without a word. There was no reason to keep it any longer. I nodded slowly, which was intended to leave the impression that I agreed with what was written. At least that's what I hoped. He seemed to be waiting for this. His smile widened.

"Excellent choice, sir," he said cordially. He bowed once again, turned and started back the way he had come.

In bewilderment I watched him go. I had no idea what I'd chosen. I hadn't actually been aware that there was any choice available. How could there be a choice when there was only one line? Oh, well, in any event I'd hidden my ignorance.

The man disappeared behind a pillar into the deep shadow of one of the church's corners and then immediately reappeared. This time his footfalls were accompanied by the dull sound of rubber touching stone. He had taken several steps in my direction before I realized he was pushing a cart. Its contents instantly resolved the mystery of a moment before. A dome-shaped silver lid with a handle at the top covered a large plate. Next to it was a silver bucket; out of it protruded the neck of a bottle wrapped in a white napkin.

I should have guessed what was going on by the place set at the table before me. It couldn't have been laid there just for the sake of decoration. If that had escaped me, the way my former boatman was now dressed should have opened my eyes. Indeed, who but a waiter in a fancy restaurant wears a green jacket with a matching bow tie? It was, of course, highly inappropriate to transform a church into a restaurant, but aren't hidden camera episodes famous for just such turnabouts? At least the more extravagant ones. Nothing was taboo.

As I watched him approach, two conflicting emotions filled me. Regardless of the fact that this wasn't a real church, I still felt uncomfortable eating in it. Some things are simply not done, particularly since this would be shown to the public. Afterwards, who would want the services of an undertaker who acted so disrespectfully towards a holy place? Would anyone go to a dentist they'd seen knock someone's teeth out in a street fight? On the other hand, my mouth had started to water at the very thought of food. Other than the slice of bread on the tram and the unfortunate sandwich in the taxi, I hadn't had a bite to eat since morning. My stomach had already started to growl in the zoo, but I'd pretended to ignore it.

When the waiter stopped next to me with his cart, the smell of food that reached my nostrils in spite of its being covered turned the tide. Elementary instincts outweighed higher considerations. I had to eat. Later I would deal with the undesirable consequences. I would try to convince the hidden camera people to leave out that scene. It certainly shouldn't mean that much to them. They had plenty of other material. If necessary, I'd threaten to sue them for tarnishing my professional reputation. I stared with hungry eyes as a white glove took hold of the top of the cover and began to raise it.

What I saw underneath almost ruined my appetite. Lying on the silver plate was some kind of baked fish. I've never been fond of fish because of my aversion to the bones, among other things, even when they are carefully prepared fillets. But ever since I'd bought the aquarium I'd stopped eating fish completely. Indeed, how would it look if I ate the same creatures I expected to give me peace of mind? I wouldn't exactly be eating the tropical fish I watched, of course, but I'd still feel uncomfortable eating other members of their species.

As I watched the waiter adroitly make a sideways cut in the flat body, turn over the top half, and then carefully extract the long spine with all its bones, I regretted the fact that there was no garnish. If there had been potatoes and greens, which are usually served with such an entrée, I would have satisfied my hunger with them and crumbled the fish to make it look like I'd tried it. Even a bit of bread would have served the purpose. But the plate only contained three thin slices of lemon that now lay beneath the overturned top of the fish.

Nothing remained but for me to eat the fish the waiter had now placed before me on the porcelain plate. What excuse could I give to get out of eating it? If I didn't even touch what I'd ordered, I would leave the impression of being overfastidious. It would be even worse if I tried to explain that I actually hadn't been aware of what I was ordering. This would only deepen the already bad impression this man must have of me, particularly after that embarrassment in the canal. I might have been able to complain about the quite limited choice he'd offered me on the menu or say that, strictly speaking, I hadn't actually ordered anything, at least not explicitly. But it was too late for that now. In any case, I might even like it. The meal appeared to be quite tastefully prepared, and my empty stomach made it easier to fight any aversion I had towards fish.

I had already reached for the knife and fork when the waiter coughed discreetly. I gave him an inquiring look. He took the bottle of wine out of the bucket of ice, turned it slightly to the side, and fiddled a bit with the cork. After removing it, he wiped the opening and then poured just a finger of wine. This was a new predicament. I would somehow be able to eat the fish, but not drink the wine. By no means. I'd only tried it once in my life and had felt nauseous after the very first sip. Since then I'd avoided even its smell. Now, however, there was no way to refuse this drink. Fish went with wine and nothing else, and there was no getting around it. If I rejected it and asked for something else, I would look like a real boor.

Luckily, though, I could pretend. I took the glass and brought it to my lips. I pressed my lips together tightly and stopped breathing. I tipped it as though taking a drink and held it in that position for a moment, ensuring that nothing dripped down the side. Then I put it back on the table at a distance. As I had allegedly tried it, I raised the napkin to wipe off the traces of liquid around my mouth. I didn't take another breath until this was done, and then nodded at the waiter.

Although he had been watching me closely, he didn't suspect a thing. He promptly filled my glass almost to the top. Then he returned the bottle to the ice bucket and put it on the table. Nothing obliged me to reach for the wine again. He would find an untouched glass when he cleared the table after the meal. He would probably think that strange, but I doubted he would venture to ask me anything. If he did, I would dream up an appropriate reply. I could also leave the question unanswered. By that time it wouldn't make any difference anyway.

"Enjoy your meal, sir," said the waiter. He bowed briefly once again and then withdrew to the corner of the church.

When the sound of his footsteps and the cart wheels had died away, I cautiously put a small piece of fish in my mouth. It was very tasty. This would have been my opinion even if I hadn't been extremely hungry. They could have given me an improvised film set meal where the quality of the dish is judged by the expression on the actor's face, but they hadn't. I had to commend the hidden camera organizers. They had really made an effort, although I didn't know why. Either they had a fantastic cook in the studio canteen or they had brought it from an expensive fish restaurant, which seemed much more probable. Too bad they hadn't asked me about my favorite food. But that, of course, was impossible. And in any case how could they have known that I don't like fish? I didn't have the right to be so picky. Such a gift horse was not to be looked in the mouth.

The idyll evaporated at the third mouthful. Carried away by the irresistible flavor, enriched with spices I had never tried before, I'd put the fact out of my mind that this was nonetheless fish. I had relied too much on the waiter, convinced that he'd done a thorough job. It seems, however, that it was impossible to remove all the bones. The tip of my tongue pushed out the one that had pricked my palate. I took it in two fingers and gave it a look. It was quite a small one, but even those could cause serious trouble. I had to be careful. I continued to eat, first cutting each piece of fish into tiny pieces with my knife and fork, and then searching for any hidden bones. This slowed me down and didn't satisfy the urge to ease my hunger as soon as possible, but I didn't dare take this lightly.

I'd eaten about one-third of the fish when the show started. A terrible draft began to blow, as if someone had opened lots of doors and windows. Had I been outside, I would have said a storm was brewing. They must have turned on powerful fans that were hidden somewhere. I didn't hear any mechanical sound, but that wasn't strange. Such studios are no doubt furnished with silent equipment. The candles blew out at almost the same moment. They went out in such unison that it seemed like someone had switched them off simultaneously. The torches held out a bit longer but went out one by one;

their flames undulated and resisted, but finally had to give way before the gusts of wind.

If I hadn't been in the middle of a meal, I wouldn't have been so bothered by the lack of originality. I was already quite used to being left in the dark sooner or later in each scene. But it was really inconsiderate of them to do it while I was eating. Couldn't they have waited a little longer for me to finish? They knew perfectly well how hungry I must be, through their fault not mine. What was the hurry, anyway? Nothing, of course. They'd been forcing me to hurry ever since the very first invitation, and afterward it had turned out there was plenty of time. I'd idled away almost a whole hour in the used bookstore before something finally happened, after I'd put my life on the line speeding to get there.

Well, I wasn't going to let them string me along anymore. If they were inconsiderate, I would be too. I would continue to eat as though the episode hadn't begun. They could go ahead and judge me as mannerless. I didn't care. First I'd consented to eat fish after so many years and then I was supposed to leave it just when it was most delicious. On starting to feel about the invisible plate in front of me with my fork, however, I realized I would have to wait a bit longer. If I'd been served anything else, the darkness wouldn't have been much of an obstacle, but how could I remove the bones without seeing what I was doing? In any case, this darkness shouldn't last very long before they raised the curtain.

And indeed, it didn't. Just as this thought crossed my mind, a bright, bluish spotlight flashed on. If I hadn't been conscious of the fact that I was in a studio, I would have been awestruck. The beam came down from the very top of the large dome in the middle of the church. It fell at something of a slant and illuminated a circle about a meter and a half in diameter on the flagstone floor to the left of the table. There was something glittering inside it, like countless little sparks going on and off. I could easily imagine a believer seeing this as a divine apparition.

The spot lit by the beam on the floor was not empty. The mostly beige-colored pile in it seemed to have fallen down from somewhere. Nothing moved for several moments. I'd just started picking through the fish, looking for bones, even though I couldn't see very well in the gloom that now surrounded me, when the pile suddenly moved. Bewildered, I laid my knife and fork on my plate. Some things were detaching themselves, like telescopic extensions. They had already almost completely emerged when I suddenly realized they were in fact limbs. And then the head rose up.

Her hair was now somewhat longer and wavy. She seemed to attract the sparks and they flocked towards her, their flickering intensifying. I had recently seen her in a swimsuit, so I knew she had a nice figure. The light-colored leotard hugging her body emphasized her slender build even more. It was revealed to the fullest when she straightened up all the way, rose onto her toes and extended her arms upward, just like the ballerina from the two drawings on the menu. Although I no longer felt the draft, the light tutu fluttered around her. Nothing was bared, yet it was extremely erotic.

She stayed in that position long enough to make it clear she was quite skilled. The girl was obviously multitalented. I'd already seen her as an actress and flautist, and now she was a ballerina, too. I wondered why someone with such qualities was wasting her time in a bit part in hidden camera shows. Money probably had something to do with it. What else? Anyone is for hire today if the price is right. Sadness filled me, as if I'd caught her in the street offering her young body to customers. My sorrow deepened when it occurred to me that I was in the same position. Or rather, in an even worse one. She would earn something at least, but what would I get out of this? Nothing. I was selling myself dirt cheap. I'd even been deprived of the right to eat in peace.

I returned to poking about the remains of the fish on my plate despite the fact that the girl had just started her number. I was quite impolite, but I hoped that at least she wouldn't hold it against me. I certainly wasn't doing it to slight her. Who knew what else awaited me that night; I might not have another chance to eat something. If I was exposed to strenuous exertion, I might easily collapse from hunger. In any case, I didn't ignore her completely. After putting a morsel of fish in my mouth I watched her for several moments before deboning another piece.

There was no doubt about it: she had years of dancing experience. Her technique was poised and gracious. She glided lightly and lithely, seemingly without effort even in this complicated choreography. The beam seemed to fuse with her. It followed her unfailingly, keeping her always in its spotlight. Unfortunately, I don't know much about ballet so I didn't recognize which piece this was from. Under normal circumstances it would surely be danced to music, but, strangely enough, that didn't seem to be necessary here.

I found the jumps particularly striking. Without much of a start, she would soar up high, as though the floor under her was elastic and not stone. It was almost like a trampoline. She would stay up in the air a long time, as though hesitating to return to the ground. After one such jump, when she stayed up there I thought at first it was natural. I even lowered my eyes to the plate in order to prepare a new bite. But the knife and fork didn't move. I raised my head slowly and stared at the ballerina.

She was about a meter above the floor. Judging by the smile on her face, this wasn't at all difficult. She wasn't doing anything to stay in the air. She was simply there, once again in the pose from the drawing. The casualness of her manner affected me. My initial disbelief turned into simple acceptance of the obvious. I accepted special effects in a movie the same way, regardless of how impossible they might seem. Thinking about the movies suddenly brought me to my senses. Of course! That's why this episode was being staged in a film studio. The equipment needed for a trick like this probably wouldn't fit in a real church.

Had this been just levitation, something long in the repertoire of illusionists, it wouldn't have been too complicated. What I was looking at, however, rose far above a circus attraction. I don't know how they did it, but the beam no longer reached the floor. It ended at the bottom of the girl's feet, as though cut off from that point. The space underneath it was filled with darkness. Although this went against common sense, I had no trouble accepting this truncated light. When dealing with the filmmaker's legerdemain, nothing should surprise you.

The ballerina finally came to life. She didn't change her pose, but moved to a horizontal position. The beam widened in order to illumine her whole length. She must have been well over two meters from her fingertips to the tips of her toes. She stayed that way for a moment and then started swimming in a circle. At least that's what it most reminded me of, how fish move. Her hands remained stretched above her head. Her intertwined hands formed a tiny fish head and her thumbs resembled bulging eyes. Her slightly parted feet were like the rear fins. Just a gentle undulation of her body was all she needed to start swimming. Air offered her aerodynamic shape even less resistance than water.

She first traced several slow circles on the same level and then started to rise in a spiral. Following her ascent, the beam left more and more darkness underneath her. The choreographer of this number must have been someone who watched fish in an aquarium as I did. Although fish most often swim chaotically, they sometimes make unexpectedly orderly maneuvers. One of these was just such a spiraling movement up or down. I'd never been able to fathom what caused it, but would venture to say it was some kind of excitement.

When she reached approximately halfway to the top of the dome, the girl suddenly stopped, as though frightened by something. Shudders coursed through her body.

When she started to swim again, her movement had lost its former regularity. She jerked and twitched, just like an agitated fish. She seemed to be trying to evade some danger, but there was limited room to escape. She tried to break through the lower edge of the beam, without success, just as fish in an aquarium are unable to go deeper than the glass at the bottom. Her lateral movements were also blocked. She went from one side to the other but seemed to run into invisible glass walls that pushed her away.

The beam continued its inexorable shortening, confining her more and more. She was now thrashing about wildly, as though caught in a net, making feverish efforts to elude the inevitable: being pulled into the circular source of light. I didn't understand her aversion until the striking similarity hit me like a shock. The upper opening resembled a wide-open mouth. A little bit more and she would be eaten.

The bite I'd chewed had just gone down my throat. The wave of guilty conscience that surged over me made me try to keep it from going down, but it was too late. I held it briefly somewhere midway, but this only made me choke, as though I'd missed a little bone in spite of my careful filleting. My breath turned to a rattle and my eyes started to water. I reached for the glass without much thought, but at the last moment realized that wine would only make things worse.

As I tried to regain my composure without water, the air ballet high above me was reaching a climax. When she was already quite close to the top of the dome, the girl fish stopped resisting, as though resigned to her fate.

176

Carried by the exertion of her previous movements, she turned languidly in a circle, its center around her navel. For some reason her submission stopped the beam from rising. The only thing that disturbed the tense silence was my raspy cough. This made me feel as uncomfortable as if it were happening at a real ballet performance. I could almost sense the reproachful glances of the audience. But then came the finale and I was released from my misery. What was left of the beam was whisked into the opening, sucking everything after it except the darkness.

How contemptible. First they starve me to death for hours. Then, after finally deigning to give me a chance to eat something, in the middle of the meal they make everything I've put in my mouth turn my stomach. Why did they have to do that? Couldn't they think of something less perverse and cruel? How would I be able to look the little fish in the eyes when I returned home? I felt for the plate in front of me and pushed it away in disgust. It seems I did it more energetically than I should have. Out of the darkness came the ringing sound of something falling.

I knew right away what had happened. The glass of wine had tipped over and spilled. Had circumstances been otherwise, I would have been mortified at this clumsiness. I'd ruined the enormous tablecloth. Now, however, I wasn't the least bit sorry. It served them right, they deserved to be a little on the receiving end. Hey, what was a tablecloth to such an expensive hidden camera episode? In any case, if the matter of compensation arose, I could always clear myself by saying that I hadn't ordered any wine; it had been forced on me, so to speak. Like the fish. Who writes menus in a foreign language? Finally, why had they turned out the lights? If they hadn't left me in the dark, I wouldn't have knocked over the glass.

The sound of footsteps echoed to my left once again. I turned in that direction, but my vision floundered in the darkness—of course the waiter didn't seem to be bothered by it. The sounds he made indicated he was heading for me. He didn't stop until he was right next to me. I didn't hear anything for several moments, although I had the impression he was doing something. I was terrified. I didn't expect him to harm me, but I still would have felt better if I could see him. Suddenly something cracked and flashed right next to my face.

I jumped back, reflexively raising my hands to protect myself. But it was unnecessary. No danger threatened me. I lowered my hands in shame. What had seemed like a flash was soon brought within modest proportions: the flame of a lighted match. The illuminated white glove moved from my side to the candlestick closest to me on the table. One after another, five tall candles received his flickering gift. As the lighting improved, the damage I'd done became all the more obvious.

I was just about to say something in my defense when the waiter raised the glass without a word, wiped it down with the napkin he'd brought, which lay across his bent arm, and then used the napkin to cover the wine stain. He then placed the glass in front of me where the plate had been. Finally, he took the bottle out of the silver bucket and poured me some more wine. The discomfort

I felt suddenly turned to irritation. This guy was really persistent. He simply couldn't get it through his head that I wasn't about to take even a sip of wine. What did I have to do to make this clear? I toyed with the idea of spilling the wine again, this time not by accident but to make a point. I didn't do it, though. Such outbursts aren't like me. I would simply ignore the wine, as though it wasn't there. If the waiter intended to stand there until I finished it, he would have a nice wait in store.

That wasn't his intention, however. He didn't return to the left-hand corner of the church as he had before, either. Walking slowly, he made his way to the other end of the table. Since only one candlestick was alight, he was swallowed up by the darkness just a few steps from me. His footsteps continued for some time longer and when they stopped it was hard to estimate the invisible distance, so I wasn't sure how far he'd gotten or why he'd stopped.

Both quandaries were cleared up when he struck another match. He was at the other end of the table, where he lit the candles on the last candlestick. As the illumination gradually increased, the contours of someone sitting there, opposite me, became more and more visible. The distance was too great to make out very much, and the broad hat brim on her bowed head completely hid her face, but I didn't have to see well to guess who it was.

This time she was dressed in white, contrasting vividly with the gloom around her. I felt my heartbeat quicken like a schoolboy's. It wasn't out of surprise, since I'd expected her to appear. I'd been part of this hidden camera sequence long enough to know that she always appeared at the end of an episode, if only as a voice. I even had a good idea where I would see her. Who else would they have set the table for down there?

After lighting the last candle, the waiter slowly headed back. He stopped when he reached me, then picked up the wine bucket and the plate of uneaten fish. I gestured with my hand that he could take the full glass too, but he paid no attention. He just turned and left. Had this been a fancy restaurant I would have summoned the maître d' at once and complained about the personnel's intolerable, even rude behavior. But I had no one to complain to here.

When the sound of his footsteps subsided, the lady in white finally moved. She stood up from her chair without raising her head. I did the same without a moment's hesitation. I had no idea what she intended to do, but good manners wouldn't let me remain seated, particularly since no danger threatened me. She reached for the glass in front of her and raised it. Candlelight danced in reflection on the crystal. I had to follow her example once more, although unwillingly. It wasn't hard to deduce what would come next, and that put me in a very awkward situation.

The hat began arching upward, like a white sunflower following the invisible sun. I leaned forward slightly over the table, even though I knew it would be of little use. She was too far away for me to get a good look at her in that light. So that had been the purpose of the long table: her face would remain hidden from me, even when the brim of her hat no longer concealed it. But the old frustration had no time to rekindle inside me because at that moment she raised her glass to her lips.

What could I do but raise my own glass? How could I refuse to reciprocate a lady's toast? That was out of the question, of course. On the other hand, it was also out of the question to take even a sip of wine. It could easily make me throw up everything I'd just eaten. What a pretty sight that would be. I started to search in panic for a way out of the trap I'd fallen into.

For a moment I thought of repeating what I'd done a little while before when the waiter had stood next to me, waiting for the go-ahead signal on the wine. I would pretend to drink. Regrettably, something like that would have been possible with just a little bit of liquid in the glass, but not now that it was full. As soon as I tipped it, keeping my mouth shut, the wine would start streaming down my cheeks. In addition, there had been no dishonor in deceiving a waiter, but I certainly couldn't act that way towards a lady.

She tipped the glass and started to drink. I thought I was at the end of my rope, when a solution suddenly occurred to me. It wasn't exactly elegant, but what other choice did I have? I would take the wine into my mouth but not swallow it. There would be complications with this alternative, too, but less than if I actually drank the wine. Hopefully I would be able to keep it in my mouth until I found a chance to spit it out somewhere. It wouldn't be easy, but I was ready to put up with just about anything to get out of this mess. I closed my eyes and took a long sip.

I hadn't intended to keep my eyes closed very long, but the disgusting taste made me do it. My face was that of a child who has been forced to swallow cod liver oil. I fervently hoped that the great distance between us was now working in my favor and she hadn't been able to see the grimace. With strenuous efforts, I finally managed to put a more-or-less normal expression on my face, but I couldn't remove all the traces of duplicity. My bulging cheeks continued to give me away. Luckily, that should have been even less visible at the other end of the table. She would be more likely to notice that my eyes were closed than the fact that my mouth was full. I quickly opened my eyes.

What I beheld brought me both frustration and relief. Or rather, what I didn't behold. There was no one facing me at the other end of the table. The candles illuminated an empty chair. I'd been outwitted once again, this time by my own fault. If I hadn't closed my eyes, she wouldn't have been able to disappear unobserved. What would they have done if I'd been a wine lover, which was much more likely? There are far more wine enthusiasts than there are people with zero tolerance for wine. They had no way of knowing I was one of the latter. They certainly must have had something prepared, but had jumped at this chance that dropped into their laps.

Although her persistent evasions made me feel foolish, they had one effect now. No considerations with regard to decent behavior prevented me from getting rid of the horrid liquid in my mouth. They might still be filming me, but I didn't care. They'd filmed me in worse predicaments than this. My reputation had already deteriorated to the point where I couldn't do much else to make it worse. The most pressing matter was to get rid of the wine.

I brought the glass to my mouth again. The best thing seemed to be to put it back inside. Actually, no other solution crossed my mind. I couldn't spit it out on the church floor, could I, even if the church was fake. Before I managed to do anything, however, someone cleared their throat next to me. Just like a child caught with his hand in the cookie box, I quickly lowered the glass and turned to my left. I knew from the sound that I would see the waiter there, but I never expected to find someone else with him.

Quite a lot seemed to have happened while I couldn't see. My eyes had been closed but not my ears. Why hadn't I heard the sound of his footsteps, since they'd always been audible before? And not one set of footsteps this time, but two? It was beyond me. They must have used some sort of trick. The ballerina was next to the waiter now, but she was no longer wearing a leotard. She too was wearing a dark-green jacket and bow tie. The only difference was that she had a medium length black skirt instead of pants. Her coiffure had not changed.

If I had been demoted from a ballerina to a waitress I would have been devastated, but it didn't seem to bother her. She smiled broadly, and so did her colleague. I tried to smile back, which wasn't easy with a mouth full of wine. I was cornered. If they asked me anything, I would have no other recourse than to swallow the liquid, regardless of the consequences. I stared at them fixedly, expecting the worst. But neither one addressed me.

183

Instead, after several frozen moments, the waiter extended his hand. Surprised, I hesitated briefly before I accepted it. I didn't know what this was supposed to mean. Was he congratulating me on something or saying goodbye? I didn't know of any reason for congratulation, and such warmth was quite unexpected from a waiter when the guest was about to leave. His grasp was firm and the handshake went on for some time. At the end he even put his other hand over our joined ones.

Then it was the girl's turn. Not until then did I realize she was holding my coat and hat. I was actually surprised that I wasn't wearing them, although, of course, it would have been foolish to keep them on at the table. First she handed me my hat, and after I'd put it on, she held out my coat. I stood before her completely dressed to go out, expecting her to hold out her hand too, if this was something the waiters had a habit of doing in this place. Instead, she came up to me, held me lightly by the shoulders and kissed first one cheek and then the other.

I froze while she did this. If she'd pressed just a tiny bit more, a stream of wine would have spurted unavoidably out of my mouth. Luckily, her lips touched me ever so lightly. She didn't move away at once. I realized with horror that I was supposed to return the kisses, but I didn't dare. We stood there like that, quite close to each other, for several moments. The embarrassment was so great I wished the earth would swallow me up. I couldn't even say anything in my defense. Finally, she took one step back.

I bowed my head in shame. My eyes lowered, I didn't notice immediately what they were doing. And then I felt them take me by the arm, one on each side. I went with them towards the large door of the church, only a few steps away. The waiter opened it, then made a polished gesture with his hand, pointing outside. I didn't leave right away. I looked at them inquiringly, but they only smiled in return. Everything, clearly, had already been said. I hesitated a moment, and then did the inevitable. I walked out into the darkness.

11

The darkness deepened when the door closed behind me. I had no idea where I was. I was somewhere outside, that alone was certain. I heard the intermittent drops of rain on the ground around me, and gentle gusts of wind caressed my face. If, as I assumed, the church I'd just left was only a film studio, then this might be the area surrounding it. It was odd that no lights were on. Unless, of course, they had been intentionally turned off. How did they think I was supposed to leave this place and go somewhere else when I couldn't see my hand in front of my face?

Probably the best thing was to ask them. I had already half-turned to bang on the door when I remembered that I wouldn't be able to say a thing. I first had to get rid of the wine. That took precedence over everything else. If I held onto it much longer it would be the same as if I'd swallowed it. I would feel both nauseous and intoxicated. And that was all I needed.

It seemed I'd have no trouble getting rid of it. No one was watching me and there would be no mess if I simply spat it out onto the ground. Besides, any trace would soon be washed away by the rain. I had turned aside to spit it out when I was stopped by a sudden thought. What if that was what they were waiting for? As soon as I opened my mouth, lights would flash so they could get a good picture of me. It would be a pretty sight: a tipsy undertaker who could find no better place to vomit than in front of a church. Afterwards who could prove that it wasn't a real church, that I wasn't really drunk, and that it wasn't even vomiting in the true sense of the word?

I weighed this briefly in my mind and then chose the lesser of two evils. I couldn't be certain that they were lying in wait to film me as I spat out the wine, but I knew perfectly well what would happen if I continued to keep my mouth shut. I bent over and opened it. It was only then, as the wine came out, that I realized how much I had actually sipped. At least half a glass. Indeed, I could have taken only a small, symbolic sip, but good manners required more of me. Was I to be outdone by the lady, who had taken a full swig?

The relief that filled me was not of long duration. It was confounded by the thing I'd feared all along. Before I had time to straighten up, there was a sudden flash. Luckily, it was not bright lights that had been turned on me. They weren't even electric lights. Right in front of me were two rows of little fires. They were parallel and placed at regular intervals, although the perspective made the gaps between them seem smaller as the distance grew. Judging by the pairs closest to me, the rows were about three steps apart. It was not hard to recognize what this was. Before me was a narrow, lighted path.

On taking a better look, I noticed that the fires were not set directly on the ground as I'd first thought. They were burning in shallow pans, like old-fashioned gas lights. The flame was bluish around the edges, which meant it was produced by the combustion of gases. The light created was weak but still gave me an idea of what surrounded me. Tombstones rose to the left and right of the path. I was in a cemetery, or rather in something that was supposed to look like a cemetery.

I knew these places even better than churches. I could find my way in one in total darkness, let alone in poor visibility. Yet even without seeing anything else, the gas lights along the path allowed me to conclude that I wasn't in any of the four town cemeteries. They were very different. The only explanation was that the studio went beyond the interior that I'd just left and extended to the surrounding exterior. That meant this hidden camera scene was still ongoing. But why had we just said goodbye as though it were all over? I must have gotten the wrong impression.

I started slowly down the path. The sound of the rain was joined by the scrunching gravel under my feet. After several steps, I had a sudden urge to look at the church behind me. Turning around, all I could make out in the weak light from the first pair of fires was the large door and its immediate surroundings. I'd seen firsthand that the building was long and tall, but that could not be detected from here. In any case, the church hadn't been just a backdrop. I knew there was a film studio in town, but I hadn't the slightest notion that it contained a church that appeared real to the tiniest detail.

I continued walking and looked around. I soon became aware of something that I, as an expert in the field, should have noticed right away. All the tombstones that I could see were the same size and shape, and the same gray color. In addition, they all had busts at the top.

You wouldn't come across that in a real cemetery. What kind of weird film set had required such homogeneity? Couldn't they have done something to change the set to the requirements of this hidden camera show? They should have realized that the environment in which I was seen by the viewers mattered quite a bit to me. This might lead them to the conclusion that we offer only one type of tombstone, which isn't at all the case. We offer a selection that is head and shoulders above that of our competitors. Most likely it had been too expensive to rearrange the whole cemetery for just one scene. Luckily, this drawback was not so conspicuous with the poor lighting.

The path stretched before me apparently without end. Far ahead the two edges marked by flaming spots seemed to merge. Regardless of the progress I made, I didn't get any closer to that point of convergence. The studio clearly had an enormous amount of space at its disposal. I stopped for a moment, hesitating about what to do. Had I done the right thing by heading away from the church door? What other choice did I have—to stand there until the end of time? If they'd wanted me to stay by the church, would they have lighted these fires? On the other hand, they surely didn't expect me to walk for miles. What would be the sense in doing that?

I could go back to the church, bang on the door and ask for directions, even though I had already experienced enough to know that the chances were pretty slim of anyone opening the door, let alone telling me anything. I hadn't been vouchsafed a single thing since the very beginning. But that was probably the way it had to be.

What kind of hidden camera scene would this be if the victim were aware of what was going on?

What if I simply stood there? That would force their hand. If they wanted me to be somewhere else, they'd have to make it known to me. How could they get me to move? They would probably try to frighten me, making me turn and run. What better place than a cemetery at night? If that were really their intention, they'd miscalculated a little, however. They would have to think up something considerably more convincing than the normal horror-movie fare. Maybe someone else would be frightened of ghosts, the walking dead, opening graves, and other such rubbish, but not an undertaker.

I stood between two pans of fire. Everything around me was still. All that disturbed the silence was the drizzling rain and rustling leaves in treetops that I couldn't see. The chirp of a bird came suddenly out of somewhere, followed by fluttering wings. I pulled my hat down a little more, raised the collar on my coat and put my hands in my pockets. On further reflection, I was the most frightening thing around. If someone unsuspecting were to appear, they'd be terrified at the sight of a figure standing completely still with his face covered. What normal person would be hanging around in such a place in the middle of the night? If they didn't think I was a ghost, the least they would take me for was some sort of maniac.

The minutes passed slowly, as is usually the case when nothing is happening. I wondered what time it was. I could look at my watch if I squatted down and brought my hand close to one of the bluish flames. But I didn't feel like it. I didn't care. For the first time that night

I wasn't being rushed somewhere. I should have enjoyed this lack of pressure, but strangely enough, impatience almost overwhelmed me. I began to fear that I'd misjudged the situation once again. If they didn't like the fact that I had stopped, why didn't they do something about it? How much longer would they make me wait?

As though in answer to this question, something happened that very moment. I was convinced that nothing could surprise me, but I jumped nonetheless at the sound of the bell. It was thunderous, as though it were right behind me. I didn't collect my wits until the third peal, when I realized that it was the church bell. Two more strikes passed before I understood that I didn't have to count them. There would be twelve, of course. It was the stroke of midnight. Although I couldn't stop myself from counting, when I counted the ninth strike the ringing abruptly lost all importance.

A dull glow suddenly began to spread over the tombstone to my left. The light seemed to emerge from the ground, slowly advancing upwards. It looked like some sort of pale white fluorescence. I knew that the countless tombstones that stretched all around me couldn't be made of marble, although that's what they looked like. It would have been an enormous, unnecessary expense. There was a much cheaper way to fashion a film set of a graveyard. I'd assumed they'd used Styrofoam, but I'd just been proven wrong. Styrofoam could never glow from within.

I turned all around but didn't see this happening anywhere else. Everything was as before. The flames of the gas lights, unaffected by the drizzling rain, dispelled

191

the darkness only slightly, and the ringing, having ceased, seemed to leave behind an even deeper silence. I turned my gaze back to the pedestal of the bust: the lower third was already glowing. It made me think of a cookie dipped in milk, slowly soaking up the whiteness beneath it.

When the glow was about halfway up, the lower part of the tombstone began to turn transparent. The inner light was eating away at the gray material that was supposed to imitate stone. So this must have been some kind of plastic or glass. Somewhere at the base of this block, under the ground, there must have been a reflector whose beam was gradually getting brighter. I felt disappointed. I'd been expecting something more refined and inventive at the end of the show. This was below the standard of the previous scenes. After all those special effects this seemed like the sleight of hand of a small-town magician.

Continuing to rise, the light finally reached the top of the square column, which was waist-high. An inscription appeared there, right next to the upper edge. It was carved into the block but not highlighted by a contrasting color, so it wasn't easy to make out. I had to walk to the side of the path and bend over to read it. I had no idea what might be written there. A name, perhaps. What else?

There was no name, however. All I could see were numbers. Not two years—birth and death—as is customary, but only one. The exact date, actually. Tomorrow's date. I looked at it briefly in confusion until it suddenly dawned on me. Not tomorrow's date but today's.

Midnight had just sounded. I had no time to ponder this enigma, however, because the glow had just spread from the pedestal to the bust, and what it revealed pushed every other thought from my mind.

She was not wearing the wide-brimmed hat. She was not too far away. She did not appear just for an instant. Finally I could look at her unconcealed, up close and for as long as I wanted. Or rather, her countenance sculpted in glass or plastic. The material was demeaning, but this had not bothered the anonymous sculptor. His skill likened it to the finest marble. A unique moment of beauty had been frozen in time: the exquisite well-proportioned shape of her head, the intoxicatingly seductive gaze, the elusive shadow of a smile, the wind playing in her long hair. Were she alive, this singular moment would have quickly passed.

The glow that came from inside enhanced her beauty even more. This might have been the decisive factor in the choice of material. Stone would not have been able to produce the soft radiance that had such a hypnotic effect on me. Even if I'd wanted, I couldn't have taken my eyes off the face in front of me. It was a blessing in disguise. Of all the places in the world, the last place I would have wanted to see her was on a tombstone, but if she had been standing there in flesh and blood, how could I have justified my fixed stare?

The beauty remained intact even when the dense glow started to thin out like dissipating mist, in accordance with what was happening below it. Taking on a sort of ethereal transparency, it became fragile and vulnerable. I felt that even a strong downpour would be enough to shatter the bust into smithereens. Yet it need fear nothing from me. I wouldn't even venture to touch it. Although I was no believer, it would have seemed like blasphemy.

The transparency made drops visible on the surface of the bust. They must have come from the rain, which continued incessantly. I was sorry that the umbrella in the zoo was gone. I would have opened it and held it over the bust until the rain stopped. But then the drops started to grow larger and multiply. They flowed into streaks and then joined as they ran down slowly in rivulets. I was ashamed of the comparison that crossed my mind: as though she were perspiring. But what would make her perspire? It was cold here, not hot. Perspiration, however, can come from overheating that is internal as well as external. And that's when I understood what was happening.

The light illuminating the tombstone from inside wasn't cold. On the contrary, by all indications its temperature was rising. So, then: what kind of plastic or glass would be covered with so much moisture because of heat? I'd never heard of anything of that nature. Only ice would act like that. I squinted. Of course! Ice! I should have recognized it immediately. That was by far the cheapest material. Anything else would be too expensive for such an enormous cemetery. I put out my hand and did what only a moment before had seemed unimaginable. My fingertips touched the cold wetness of her cheek.

The sudden realization of what was about to happen made me freeze as well. The heat would continue its

194

destructive work. The ice would melt more and more, destroying her beauty, turning it into ugliness, deformity. I couldn't let that happen. I had to do something. I turned around in distress, but couldn't spot anything in the empty gloom of the path and its close vicinity that would be of help.

What I finally did was the result of panic, not forethought. I bent down, grabbed the square pillar holding the bust approximately in the middle and strained with all my might. But it was just like trying to pull up a marble tombstone with my bare arms. All I managed to do was soak my coat through and through once again. The ice block was completely wet from the water pouring down it. When I finally let go and stepped back, I was totally flushed from the ineffectual effort. Despair filled me. She would meet her doom before my very eyes and I could do nothing to prevent it.

I couldn't watch anymore. I turned towards the church, intending to head quickly in that direction, maybe even run. Then I realized that that would be shameful and cowardly, just like turning my back on someone at death's door. No, I had to find the courage to stay with her until the end, as difficult as it might be. Who else was there if not me? I turned back reluctantly.

I was ready for the worst horror. It wasn't hard to imagine the beautiful proportions melting into disfiguration, the eyes turning hollow, the smile twisting into a loathsome grimace, the smooth hair turning into a tangle. But I didn't see any of this. The face, even though changed, retained its beauty. The water streaming off it

195

seemed to take away only the years. The pedestal now held the bust of a very young girl, with just a hint of the womanliness to come.

I didn't have time to be surprised at this change because the transformation was ongoing. The tombstone seemed to be a water clock that measured time backwards, faster and faster. Spellbound, I watched the maiden turn into a little girl. The head decreased proportionally in size, although not the hair, which stayed long all the while. Nothing in her expression indicated that she was suffering from this rejuvenation. On the contrary, her serenity remained untouched and the increasing internal radiation seemed to light her up with joy.

When the little girl began turning into a child of undetermined gender, her hair suddenly going short, I finally had to face full-on the question that had plagued me as soon as I'd realized what was going on. Where would this plummeting into the past end? And just as it formed in my consciousness, the force of the painfully obvious answer hit me. It wouldn't stop.

The feeling of helplessness that had just dissipated flamed up once again. I knew that there was no way I could prevent the inevitable. All that remained was to witness her disappearance when the heat no longer had anything on the pedestal to melt. This would have been easier to bear somehow if the clock were moving forward. As it was, all sense of meaning was lost. I wasn't even certain this could be called death.

The child became a baby, a transition that finally chased away the tranquil expression. The face of the little creature twisted and contracted, depicting some discomfort it was experiencing. The little mouth curled, doing its utmost to make a sound, but nothing came out. Suddenly, the brightness of the light multiplied, forcing me to squint. The ice that formed the little bald head became very thin. That fine membrane wouldn't be able to hold out much longer against the tremendous rays attacking it from within.

When one shining ray suddenly streamed outside, a cry resounded. The first cry of a newborn, just come into the world. I heard it but didn't see the lips from which it sprang. The flash forced me to close my eyes. Even then, the bright picture that remained blinded me—under tightly shut lids. When I hesitantly opened my eyes soon after, fiery white circles danced before them, blocking my view. When they finally dissipated, it was already too late. There was nothing left to see.

There was no bust on the pedestal. No light welled forth from the ground. The only trace of what had just happened was rivulets of water meandering down the icy block. But they too quickly thinned out in the cold autumn night. Although I had nothing left to do there, I stayed a while longer. Undertakers are always the last to leave a funeral. I listened to the rain as it drummed relentlessly on the gravel path, the ice tombstones, the grass between them, the leaves in the darkness. On my hat and coat. On my distraught thoughts.

When I finally left, my head was still full of jumbled thoughts, but one thing was certain. The only way back was by the path that had brought me there. It at least led somewhere, while the opposite direction led far into the distance. I hadn't walked very far when the end of the path came into view. The two rows of low flaming pearls ended in one point. The distance I'd covered on the way out seemed longer than the way back, but that was probably a common illusion. The return always seems shorter.

When I got close to the next-to-last pair of gas lights, it turned out not to be an illusion. The path I'd taken back had truly been shorter, because it didn't lead me to the place from which I had initially set out. The light shed by the small fires was weak, but enough to realize that I wasn't in front of the church door. Instead, a tall black gate rose before me with gilded spikes at the top, continuing in both directions as a brick wall. It was made of solid metal, so I couldn't see through it.

I wasn't surprised. The time for surprises was behind me. I wasn't even surprised when I recognized the gate. The fact that I couldn't see through it wasn't an obstacle. I knew perfectly well what was on the other side. I went up, grabbed the large knob, and pushed. Had circumstances been normal, my attempt to leave would have been in vain, because the gate is always locked at night. But the circumstances were anything but normal.

The large gate opened without a sound. I walked out and closed it behind me. I found myself in a street that was not new to me. Far from it. I've been coming here every day in the morning and leaving late in the afternoon for more than thirty years. Behind the black gate is the funeral parlor where I work, and one of the city cemeteries. Not very big, with nothing unusual about it. What, in any case, can be unusual about a cemetery?

Marble tombstones of different shapes and sizes, a rose garden to place the urns, cypresses, lawns, asphalt paths. Wreaths and flowers. And the solemn tranquility of death. Especially at night, when the locked gate keeps life out. I needed nothing to convince me that the same thing had happened just now.

There was no reason to stay there at this late hour. Particularly since I had one more thing to do before I went to bed: to make a visit that would allow no delay. If someone had told me just a few hours ago where I would be heading after midnight, I wouldn't have hesitated to call them a lunatic. Now I was in a hurry to get there as soon as possible, in the faint hope that it would help me hold onto my own sanity. I briskly set off down the street.

12

It took a good half hour of walking fast to reach my destination. I met almost no one on the way. Had it not been for the few cars that quickly passed me by, I might have thought I was moving through a dead city. The rain stopped soon after I set out, leaving behind a silent night disturbed only by my footsteps splashing along the wet pavement and heavy drops falling from the trees. I didn't even try to collect my thoughts. Even so, I couldn't prevent some of the previous evening's images from returning. They appeared at random, like a series of unconnected pictures. Or at least I was unable to make any sense out of them.

They weren't the main events but certain details that I'd had no obvious reason to remember. They popped up quite vividly, building a colorful mosaic. The sleeve that I tried to pull my hand through as it held the piece of bread I was eating; the eyes of the dead actors and actresses that chased me out of the Film Archives' foyer; lurching about in the back seat of the taxi while trying to eat a sandwich without being noticed; taking books out of the crammed shelves while standing at the top of the ladder in the secondhand bookstore; the rhythmic changing of the traffic light at the distant intersection on the empty city street; the row of yellow arrows on the path that led me through the zoo; the two symmetrical waterfalls pouring into the dirty water of the underground canal; the mirror in the cramped elevator creating four illusions of infinity; the cutlery viewed from an unusual angle on the table in the church; the large, dark pebbles covering the path in the cemetery.

The entrance to the maternity hospital was brightly lit. I stood in the shadow of a linden across the street for a while, hesitating. Impatience urged me to hurry, but reluctance still held me back. This was the only place I dared hope to get some answers, yet I simply couldn't think of the right questions to ask. Everything that came to mind sounded insane. If my inkling proved mistaken, the prospects were grim. I would be thrown out as soon as I said why I'd come. The obstetrician already considered me to be of unsound mind, so I actually had nothing to lose. It made no difference if his opinion of me dropped another notch. I headed across the street.

Everything in the reception hall was bathed in neon. I expected to be struck by a terrible hospital smell, but instead was met by a sweet, artificial odor. I didn't know what a maternity hospital looked like at night, but still I imagined I would find someone there, although maybe not a crowd. People die all the time in a large city, which meant that births should be just as frequent. But there was no one in the large hall. To my right was a long counter with no one behind it. There was nobody to my left either, in the row of white plastic chairs with blue cushions. In the middle of the wall facing me, decorated with framed children's drawings, was the wide door to the elevator.

I stopped for a moment at the entrance, confused by the absence of even a nurse at the counter. What if a woman about to give birth had appeared instead of me?

Whom would she turn to? Who would sign her in? This was quite objectionable and even dangerous. Perhaps the nurse had just stepped out for a moment? Anyone might experience the need for a brief absence. Even so, such places shouldn't be left without someone on permanent duty. A replacement should have been found. Such was the case in funeral parlors. Indeed, what would it look like if a customer who needed funeral services were to appear and found no one? They would head for the competition at once. Here, of course, there was no alternative. No one is in a hurry to go to a funeral, but deliveries permit no delay. A woman might give birth while on the way to another maternity hospital.

Not knowing what else to do, I headed for the counter. I would wait for the nurse. Actually, when I thought it over, her absence was a blessing in disguise. I had a greater aversion toward talking to whomever was on duty at the registration desk than to running into the doctor again. I didn't know what to say or how to act so as not to arouse suspicion. They would surely look at me askance when I said I wanted to see the duty obstetrician. I would be in a mess if they asked why. Someone like me obviously didn't need their professional services. All I could do was to say it was a private visit, but the late hour would make that a not very convincing excuse. This way I could cut short her excessive curiosity. I would give her such a reproachful look for leaving the counter that it wouldn't occur to her to inquire into my reasons.

The minutes dragged by slowly and still no one appeared. At one point I peered behind the counter apprehensively, but found nothing unusual: a lit computer monitor, a keyboard, a half-empty cup of coffee, a little vase with several wild flowers, a large barrette, an open book, a telephone with lots of buttons, two quarters of an apple on a plate. I stayed there a little while longer, and then fatigue got the upper hand. There was no reason to wait for the nurse while standing.

I went to the chairs facing the counter and sat down on one of them. When the duty nurse finally deigned to return to the post she certainly should not have left for so long, the way I walked towards her would clearly show what I thought of her inadmissible behavior. I'd just settled in the chair, feeling instant relief in my aching feet, when a humming sound broke the silence of the reception hall.

I couldn't tell where it was coming from right away. It seemed as though someone had turned on the hospital's PA system. I looked around, but couldn't see a loudspeaker anywhere. It was only when the elevator door started to open that I realized what it was. I got up at once, hoping that my body language would successfully express bitterness and impatience. But there was no one to impress. There was no one behind the sliding elevator door.

I stared into the empty depths of the elevator. It was quite spacious and obviously used to transport patients on gurneys. One other thing distinguished it from the little elevator I'd taken about two hours before: there were no mirrors. The three bare walls were painted olive green, and the floor and ceiling were of the same color. Two long florescent lights brightly illuminated the interior. I stood there staring into it, waiting, as though someone might miraculously materialize.

No one appeared, of course, but the door didn't close. About one minute passed before I realized it was senseless to keep standing there. Nothing would happen. I could go and sit down again. But I didn't. I headed slowly towards the elevator and stopped two paces in front of it. To an observer I must have appeared like some kind of savage who'd never seen such a device before, and was now inspecting it warily.

The scene was all the more comic owing to the fact that there was absolutely nothing to see inside. The only detail that broke the drab, depressing walls was the vertical row of buttons with floor numbers. They should have all been off since the elevator was standing still, but they weren't. For some reason the large square designating the second floor was lit. I couldn't figure this out. What would happen, I wondered, if I were to enter the elevator? Would it take me to the second floor?

There was only one way to find out. It took a while to go in, however. The savage was in no rush to negotiate the last two paces, and lingered at the threshold for quite some time, unwilling to take the plunge, as though facing the wide open jaws of a hungry monster. I finally made the last step across the narrow opening that separated the floor of the reception hall from the floor of the elevator. As soon as I did so, the two halves of the door rushed to meet each other, joining without a sound right behind my back.

My first instinct was to turn around in panic and try to open the door by force. There was no time for that, however, as the elevator started moving as soon as the door closed. This time the humming was of short duration and I barely felt it when the elevator stopped. The door opened behind me, but I didn't rush out. On the contrary, I stayed there with my back turned to whoever was outside the elevator, not even daring to turn around.

Considerable willpower was needed to overcome the terrified savage in me. I finally turned around slowly and faced the space in front of the open door. The part of the corridor I could see was illuminated solely by the elevator. The wall opposite me was the same olive green as the elevator's inside. I wondered why they hadn't chosen a more cheerful color for the place where we come into this world. Our first impressions are very important. The only object within my field of vision was an enormous pot containing a tall rubber plant with lots of branches.

I peered to the left and right before going out. The corridor led in both directions, but was almost totally dark. There was just one light above a door some distance down the corridor to the left. The prospect of exchanging the brightly lit elevator for the unknown dark corridor on the second floor wasn't very appealing, but what else could I do? Return to the ground floor and keep waiting for the nurse? That could easily take some time and once she appeared I would probably have to go into a laborious explanation, regardless of how angry I seemed. Now I was at least spared that.

Another possibility would be to go up to a better lit floor and look for someone to ask where to find the obstetrician on duty. Yes, but which one? The building had twelve floors, and I had no idea where to look first. I would only look suspicious if someone found me taking the elevator at random. This was a maternity hospital, after all, someone couldn't just walk in off the street and wander around wherever they wanted. Besides, why should I go any further? There must be someone on this floor. And as far as darkness was concerned, so much had happened since this started that I'd become practically insensitive to it. So why should I be frightened of an ordinary hospital corridor without any lights?

When the elevator door closed after I stepped out, however, my self-confidence evaporated into thin air. The faintly illumined rubber plant had a part in this, as it had now turned into a threatening shape with raised limbs. I quickly moved away from it in the only direction I could go—towards the glowing bulb, which now seemed farther away than when I first saw it. As I walked towards it, an unpleasant prickling sensation at the back of my neck urged me to turn around, but I didn't succumb.

I didn't know where I was heading. There certainly had to be a reason why only this door was lit. It might be the room of the head nurse of the ward on the second floor, but this was just a guess. I knew very little about maternity hospitals. The last time I'd been in one was when I was born, something both long ago and, naturally, completely beyond my recollection.

The doors I passed on both sides of the hall had no designation except numbers. They were large enough to read even in the faint light. Before I reached the door under the lightbulb, I noticed that it differed from the others. The plate on it was not square. The inscription on the narrow rectangle was too small to read from a distance even though it was well illuminated. I could only read it when I stopped in front of the door.

My first thought was that I was in luck. But then an inner voice reminded me that I'd never been on good terms with fortune. In addition, luck only appears where chance holds sway, and what had been happening to me since the previous afternoon was anything but chance. Nothing here in the maternity hospital was accidental either. Neither the empty reception hall, nor the elevator bringing me to the second floor, nor the fact that I was now standing in front of a door with the inscription "Obstetrician on Duty."

The voice of reason piped up again inside, advising me to leave before it was too late. Whatever awaited me behind this door might be something I ought not know. I had been brought there by reckless, excessive curiosity, and that often proves fatal. Sometimes ignorant bliss is better than unwanted knowledge. The smartest thing would be simply to turn around, go back to the elevator, descend to the ground floor, leave the maternity hospital, return home and go to bed. When I woke up in the morning, it would all seem like a strange dream. I might even forget it over time, just as I'd forgotten other dreams. The voice inside me was right, of course. In all respects except one. It was too late to back out. I knocked on the door.

There was no reply. Maybe they hadn't heard. The knock had indeed echoed down the empty corridor, but if the door was padded on the inside, this would muffle the sound. I knocked louder, looking up and down the corridor uncomfortably. The noise I'd made wasn't at all suited to the peaceful night of the maternity hospital. Again no one replied from within. I hesitated a few moments, then did something that in normal circumstances would have looked almost like breaking and entering: I took hold of the door handle and slowly pushed.

As it curved downwards, I hoped that the door would be locked. That would spare me considerable embarrassment. Then I could even leave with a clear conscience. I hadn't held back in a cowardly fashion, I'd tried everything reasonable. What else was I supposed to do? Break down the door? No one could blame me for not going as far as that. Unfortunately, the lock offered no resistance when the handle reached the bottom of its curve. The door started to move effortlessly.

I opened it a little way, then stopped. For the sake of caution I knocked again, this time on the door jamb. If the person inside were sleeping they might not have heard my previous knock, but they certainly couldn't miss this. I waited a bit. There was no sound inside the office. I opened the door a little more and stuck my head in hesitantly.

One look was enough to see that the room was empty. Good manners dictated that I now withdraw, but instead I slipped inside and closed the door behind me. This was no time for considering good manners. Of all the worries that plagued me, the least was that I might be reproached for entering a room where I had no right to be. On the contrary, in fact. This was exactly where I ought to be. I'd been on an extremely winding path for hours and it had led right there.

I looked around me. The atmosphere was not at all that of a hospital. This could have been the office of a professor of literature. The two side walls were completely covered with bookshelves. I had no idea that there were so many books on obstetrics. Perhaps they weren't professional books? It was hard to read the titles from a distance, but judging by the variety of the book spines they could easily have been fiction. The doctor doubtless had plenty of free time between births and interventions, and passed the time reading. What else could he do? There was no television in the room.

A window filled most of the opposite wall. White gauzy curtains bordered by heavy drapes let in the weak orangey glow of the city night. Had the lighting in the room been stronger it would have been subdued, but the only source of light was on the solid wood desk, a lamp with an oval green plastic cover. The desk was in front of the window and the few objects upon it were tidily placed. The cone-shaped beam of the lamp shone on writing implements: a brown leather blotter, a large open notebook, and a pencil holder with pens and pencils sticking out like disproportionately long quills on the back of a small, square hedgehog without a head.

A pen was lying across the notebook, indicating that the doctor had recently been writing. Something had apparently interrupted him. I didn't suppose it was an official document. Such things are written on a typewriter or computer, not by hand. The table held

209

neither of these machines, however. So the obstetrician not only loved literature, but wrote it as well. Why not? I've always been irritated by the preconceived notion that people from other fields shouldn't try their hand at literature. Doctors, for example. Or undertakers.

I had nothing more to do there. I could have sat in one of the two leather armchairs facing the desk and waited for the doctor to return, but it didn't seem wise. Not because I would feel like an uninvited guest, but because I suspected no one would come. As I turned towards the door to leave, something crossed my mind. I stole back towards the desk like a thief, went around it and sat down. Just as my eyes dropped to the page half-filled with tiny, slanted writing, there came a knock at the door.

I jumped out of my seat. In the first moment of complete confusion, "Come in!" almost slipped out. I bit my tongue to stop myself from saying anything and turned around feverishly, trying to find somewhere to hide. If it were the obstetrician, of course, I'd have no reason to hide, but he wouldn't knock at the door to his own office. It must be one of the medical staff, and it would be quite irregular if I were to be found inside. I would never be able to offer a simple and satisfactory explanation as to why I was there, far less why I was now standing behind the doctor's desk.

My first thought was to slip behind the drapes. That's what they do in the movies. But this wasn't a movie, where everything is perfect. Even though the drapes were heavy, they were too narrow to conceal me properly. Panic had already started to set in, when it dawned on me that there was a suitable hiding place right in front of me. I quickly crouched down behind the desk. Just as my head descended below the thick glass covering the desk, I heard the door open. I held my breath.

The silence of the grave reigned for several moments. I didn't know what was happening on the other side of the desk. My only hope was that the person who had come in looking for the obstetrician on duty would leave after verifying that he wasn't there. I would be in a mess if they decided to wait for him. I couldn't crouch there indefinitely without moving. Sooner or later a noise would give me away and I'd be in real trouble. But then I heard the sound of the door closing at the other side of the room.

I didn't dare breathe just yet. What if the person hadn't left but was still in the office and had just closed the door? This wasn't very probable, but couldn't be ruled out entirely. I pricked up my ears, but there was nothing to be heard. After some time I realized I had no choice. I couldn't stay there forever. I had to take the risk. Putting the palms of my hands on the thick carpet, which was of the same dark red as the drapes, I peered very cautiously around the side of the desk. I would be hardest to spot down there because the desk cast a shadow.

The office was empty. I didn't get up right away, however. Just to be on the safe side, I crawled on all fours around the side of the desk and only stood up when I reached the front. I hastened to the door on tiptoe and put my ear against it. Luckily it wasn't padded as I'd assumed. I stayed there like that for a long time, but could hear nothing on the other side. I finally concluded that I had to take another risk. I didn't dare hesitate. The sooner I left the office the better.

I'd already grabbed the handle, when a thought made me stop. I turned towards the desk and looked at the open notebook. I was suddenly torn by conflicting desires: to see what was written in it or to leave the office. I felt like a coward when the latter won out. Even the intuition that a fresh knock at the door might prevent me from reading what was written in the notebook did little to lessen the self-contempt that filled me.

It was dark outside. In the meantime someone had turned off the only light in the corridor. My intention had been to sneak out of the office, but now I wavered at the threshold. When I closed the door behind me, I would be in total darkness. This didn't appeal to me, even though it had seemed not long ago that I'd become immune to the dark, but once again necessity made the choice for me. Regardless of what was lying in wait ahead, I could no longer go back. I walked out of the office.

In spite of my expectations, the darkness wasn't total. A bit further down the corridor, part of the wall seemed to give off a muted dark-blue glow, creating a modest, artificial light. I had no idea what it could be, and no particular desire to find out. On the other hand, what else could I do but head in that direction? If I headed the other way, towards the elevator, I would soon have to grope my way along in the pitch black. So I made my way towards the blue light.

I wasn't exactly anxious to go. Dragging my feet, ears pricked, I proceeded warily, but the corridor was quiet and nothing moved. About halfway to the beginning of the blue light I discovered what it was. Part of the wall was covered with glass and the light came from the room on the other side. Though I didn't know much about maternity hospitals, it wasn't hard to figure out that this was where new fathers were brought to see their newborn offspring. In an instant I realized what was about to happen.

Instead of rushing ahead, I suddenly stopped. I remained like that for quite some time, postponing the thing that had brought me there, the reason I'd gone through everything the night before and been willing to exchange restraint for passion, prudence for imprudence, reality for unreality. The moment I would finally see her. The wild beating of my heart seemed to come not from within but from without, from all directions, multiplying as it bounced off the walls, making me deaf and threatening to rouse the whole hospital.

I couldn't allow this to happen, of course, so I continued on my way. I reached the edge of the window, but instead of looking inside, took several more steps until I was more or less in the middle. Only then did I turn. What I saw bewildered me at first. I saw her, but not only her. I saw myself too. The two shapes overlapped, suffusing each other, merging as though one. It took a few moments to realize that it was an optical illusion. I was looking at her directly, while I was just a reflection in the glass.

She was lying on her back in what must have been an incubator. The transparent sarcophagus placed right next to the window had a multitude of thin and thick tubes that connected it to an external apparatus full of different colored lights and digital numbers. She was completely naked, as newborns usually are in such places. Her head was turned to the side, towards me. Her eyes were closed. As I looked at her, I thought how strange it was. Until yesterday, I would never have been able to distinguish one baby from another. Not even older babies. Now, however, there wasn't a trace of doubt. Before me was the same tiny creature whose last or first cry still echoed in my ears.

And yet there was a difference. In the agony of dying/birthing, her face, even though made of ice, had been painfully alive. Now there was no pain, nor any reason to move. She was completely still, probably because she was asleep, but fear suddenly shot through me. I had to see at least some sign that she was alive. Although tiny, her lungs should move gently, but I couldn't see that. My reflection got in the way. I put my face right up against the glass and shielded it on both sides with my hands.

Now she was all I saw. I breathed a sigh of relief when I noted the barely visible rising and lowering of her chest. But I saw something else as well: the blissful tranquility on her face. As though this first sleep had shown her everything that was to come, all that I'd already seen in the opposite, accelerated order: growing up, becoming ever more delicate, captivating and beautiful. I lowered my eyelids so that my inner eye could see that transformation once again, just as rapidly as before but this time going in the right direction.

The last picture froze in my mind: her face no longer concealed by the hat brim, her hair scattered by the breeze, her radiant smile that filled me with immeasurable joy. I stared for a long time at this scene from a time yet to come, when I would already be a feeble old man, if I were alive at all. But I felt no sorrow. On the contrary, what filled me defied the destructive effect of time. It was a feeling of fulfillment, accomplishment, joy. A feeling of happiness.

The illusion of happiness dissipated when I suddenly realized that I'd been standing at the window too long. Someone might appear and find me in this strange position at a place where, formally speaking, I had no right to be, particularly at this late hour. Indeed, what could I say if they were to ask me my relationship to the baby? The best thing would be not to reply at all. It would be hard to stop myself from going into an explanation of a relationship that, although not a blood tie, might be even closer than that. But I dared not hope that my explanation would be met with understanding.

I stepped back from the glass and my reflection immediately overlapped with the incubator, merging with it. That was to be expected. What was not to be expected, however, was the appearance of three more reflections. They came so suddenly that surprise caused me to shiver. I stared fixedly at the three faces as though they were ghosts and not quite familiar to me. To my left were the girl and the middle-aged man I'd seen in countless roles during the previous evening. To my right was the obstetrician, and even though I'd only met him briefly once, it had been enough to remember him well. All three were looking at me in this quasi-mirror, smiling.

215

I turned slowly, suspecting what I would find, but this didn't stop me. There was no one behind me. I was facing a bare wall, its sickly olive green transformed by the blue radiance into dark purple. I felt as though I were standing on the edge of a horizontal chasm that gaped before me without end. If I didn't turn my eyes away, soon I would plunge into a dizzy vortex. But before this had a chance to happen, the purple abyss disappeared, taking everything with it. I wasn't even sure that I myself existed in the heart of darkness that engulfed me.

I couldn't tell how long the darkness lasted after the blue light went out in the incubator room. It might have been just a few moments and it might have been the better part of eternity. I stood there in the middle of nothingness, waiting. When the change finally happened, I heard it first. Somewhere far to my left there was a faint humming sound. I turned; at the bottom of the tunnel stretching before me was a small circle of light containing a pot with a small green plant. An extreme effort of imagination was needed to recognize the large pot and considerably larger rubber plant in this miniature.

The walk to the waiting elevator seemed endless. I moved forward but seemed to get no closer. I wanted to run at one point, but suppressed the instinct. I wouldn't get there any faster and it would look like I was fleeing. And I had no one to flee from. No one was chasing me. There was nothing behind me but the innocuously quiet nighttime of the maternity hospital. I was the only intruder.

Once again there was no need to push anything in the open elevator. The button for the ground floor was already lit. The door started to close quietly as soon as I entered and I turned to face it, until it finally shut out the view of the enormous plant. When it opened soon after, I squinted at the blinding florescent light in the empty reception hall. I didn't need to look to the left to ascertain that the duty nurse had still not returned. I headed straight for the exit.

Drizzling rain greeted me once again outside. I raised my coat collar and adjusted my hat a little. A long walk home was before me. I would get there sooner if I took a taxi, but the nocturnal walk would do me good, even though it would mean going to bed much later than usual. I would be sleepy at work, something a serious undertaker shouldn't allow to happen. It leaves a bad impression on the customers. But justification lay in the exceptional circumstances, and I would try to make my indisposition as unnoticeable as possible.

SELECTED DALKEY ARCHIVE PAPERBACKS

PETROS ABATZOGLOU, *What Does Mrs. Freeman Want?*
PIERRE ALBERT-BIROT, *Grabinoulor.*
YUZ ALESHKOVSKY, *Kangaroo.*
SVETLANA ALEXIEVICH, *Voices from Chernobyl.*
FELIPE ALFAU, *Chromos.*
    Locos.
IVAN ÂNGELO, *The Celebration.*
    The Tower of Glass.
DAVID ANTIN, *Talking.*
DJUNA BARNES, *Ladies Almanack.*
    Ryder.
JOHN BARTH, *LETTERS.*
    Sabbatical.
DONALD BARTHELME, *Paradise.*
SVETISLAV BASARA, *Chinese Letter.*
ANDREI BITOV, *Pushkin House.*
LOUIS PAUL BOON, *Chapel Road.*
ROGER BOYLAN, *Killoyle.*
IGNÁCIO DE LOYOLA BRANDÃO, *Zero.*
CHRISTINE BROOKE-ROSE, *Amalgamemnon.*
BRIGID BROPHY, *In Transit.*
MEREDITH BROSNAN, *Mr. Dynamite.*
GERALD L. BRUNS,
    Modern Poetry and the Idea of Language.
GABRIELLE BURTON, *Heartbreak Hotel.*
MICHEL BUTOR, *Degrees.*
    Mobile.
    Portrait of the Artist as a Young Ape.
G. CABRERA INFANTE, *Infante's Inferno.*
    Three Trapped Tigers.
JULIETA CAMPOS, *The Fear of Losing Eurydice.*
ANNE CARSON, *Eros the Bittersweet.*
CAMILO JOSÉ CELA, *The Family of Pascual Duarte.*
    The Hive.
LOUIS-FERDINAND CÉLINE, *Castle to Castle.*
    London Bridge.
    North.
    Rigadoon.
HUGO CHARTERIS, *The Tide Is Right.*
JEROME CHARYN, *The Tar Baby.*
MARC CHOLODENKO, *Mordechai Schamz.*
EMILY HOLMES COLEMAN, *The Shutter of Snow.*
ROBERT COOVER, *A Night at the Movies.*
STANLEY CRAWFORD, *Some Instructions to My Wife.*
ROBERT CREELEY, *Collected Prose.*
RENÉ CREVEL, *Putting My Foot in It.*
RALPH CUSACK, *Cadenza.*
SUSAN DAITCH, *L.C.*
    Storytown.
NIGEL DENNIS, *Cards of Identity.*
PETER DIMOCK,
    A Short Rhetoric for Leaving the Family.
ARIEL DORFMAN, *Konfidenz.*
COLEMAN DOWELL, *The Houses of Children.*
    Island People.
    Too Much Flesh and Jabez.
RIKKI DUCORNET, *The Complete Butcher's Tales.*
    The Fountains of Neptune.
    The Jade Cabinet.
    Phosphor in Dreamland.
    The Stain.
    The Word "Desire."
WILLIAM EASTLAKE, *The Bamboo Bed.*
    Castle Keep.
    Lyric of the Circle Heart.
JEAN ECHENOZ, *Chopin's Move.*
STANLEY ELKIN, *A Bad Man.*
    Boswell: A Modern Comedy.
    Criers and Kibitzers, Kibitzers and Criers.
    The Dick Gibson Show.
    The Franchiser.
    George Mills.
    The Living End.
    The MacGuffin.
    The Magic Kingdom.

    Mrs. Ted Bliss.
    The Rabbi of Lud.
    Van Gogh's Room at Arles.
ANNIE ERNAUX, *Cleaned Out.*
LAUREN FAIRBANKS, *Muzzle Thyself.*
    Sister Carrie.
LESLIE A. FIEDLER,
    Love and Death in the American Novel.
GUSTAVE FLAUBERT, *Bouvard and Pécuchet.*
FORD MADOX FORD, *The March of Literature.*
CARLOS FUENTES, *Christopher Unborn.*
    Terra Nostra.
    Where the Air Is Clear.
JANICE GALLOWAY, *Foreign Parts.*
    The Trick Is to Keep Breathing.
WILLIAM H. GASS, *The Tunnel.*
    Willie Masters' Lonesome Wife.
ETIENNE GILSON, *The Arts of the Beautiful.*
    Forms and Substances in the Arts.
C. S. GISCOMBE, *Giscome Road.*
    Here.
DOUGLAS GLOVER, *Bad News of the Heart.*
    The Enamoured Knight.
KAREN ELIZABETH GORDON, *The Red Shoes.*
GEORGI GOSPODINOV, *Natural Novel.*
PATRICK GRAINVILLE, *The Cave of Heaven.*
HENRY GREEN, *Blindness.*
    Concluding.
    Doting.
    Nothing.
JIŘÍ GRUŠA, *The Questionnaire.*
JOHN HAWKES, *Whistlejacket.*
AIDAN HIGGINS, *A Bestiary.*
    Flotsam and Jetsam.
    Langrishe, Go Down.
    Scenes from a Receding Past.
    Windy Arbours.
ALDOUS HUXLEY, *Antic Hay.*
    Crome Yellow.
    Point Counter Point.
    Those Barren Leaves.
    Time Must Have a Stop.
MIKHAIL IOSSEL AND JEFF PARKER, EDS., *Amerika:*
    Contemporary Russians View
    the United States.
GERT JONKE, *Geometric Regional Novel.*
JACQUES JOUET, *Mountain R.*
HUGH KENNER, *The Counterfeiters.*
    Flaubert, Joyce and Beckett:
    The Stoic Comedians.
DANILO KIŠ, *Garden, Ashes.*
    A Tomb for Boris Davidovich.
NOBUO KOJIMA, *Embracing Family.*
TADEUSZ KONWICKI, *A Minor Apocalypse.*
    The Polish Complex.
MENIS KOUMANDAREAS, *Koula.*
ELAINE KRAF, *The Princess of 72nd Street.*
JIM KRUSOE, *Iceland.*
EWA KURYLUK, *Century 21.*
VIOLETTE LEDUC, *La Bâtarde.*
DEBORAH LEVY, *Billy and Girl.*
    Pillow Talk in Europe and Other Places.
JOSÉ LEZAMA LIMA, *Paradiso.*
OSMAN LINS, *Avalovara.*
    The Queen of the Prisons of Greece.
ALF MAC LOCHLAINN, *The Corpus in the Library.*
    Out of Focus.
RON LOEWINSOHN, *Magnetic Field(s).*
D. KEITH MANO, *Take Five.*
BEN MARCUS, *The Age of Wire and String.*
WALLACE MARKFIELD, *Teitlebaum's Window.*
    To an Early Grave.
DAVID MARKSON, *Reader's Block.*
    Springer's Progress.
    Wittgenstein's Mistress.

FOR A FULL LIST OF PUBLICATIONS, VISIT:
www.dalkeyarchive.com

SELECTED DALKEY ARCHIVE PAPERBACKS

CAROLE MASO, *AVA*

LADISLAV MATEJKA AND KRYSTYNA POMORSKA, EDS.,
Readings in Russian Poetics: Formalist and Structuralist Views.

HARRY MATHEWS,
The Case of the Persevering Maltese: Collected Essays.
Cigarettes.
The Conversions.
The Human Country: New and Collected Stories.
The Journalist.
My Life in CIA.
Singular Pleasures.
The Sinking of the Odradek Stadium.
Tlooth.
20 Lines a Day.

ROBERT L. MCLAUGHLIN, ED.,
Innovations: An Anthology of Modern & Contemporary Fiction.

STEVEN MILLHAUSER, *The Barnum Museum.*
In the Penny Arcade.

RALPH J. MILLS, JR., *Essays on Poetry.*

OLIVE MOORE, *Spleen.*

NICHOLAS MOSLEY, *Accident.*
Assassins.
Catastrophe Practice.
Children of Darkness and Light.
The Hesperides Tree.
Hopeful Monsters.
Imago Bird.
Impossible Object.
Inventing God.
Judith.
Look at the Dark.
Natalie Natalia.
Serpent.
The Uses of Slime Mould: Essays of Four Decades.

WARREN F. MOTTE, JR.,
Fables of the Novel: French Fiction since 1990.
Oulipo: A Primer of Potential Literature.

YVES NAVARRE, *Our Share of Time.*

DOROTHY NELSON, *Tar and Feathers.*

WILFRIDO D. NOLLEDO, *But for the Lovers.*

FLANN O'BRIEN, *At Swim-Two-Birds.*
At War.
The Best of Myles.
The Dalkey Archive.
Further Cuttings.
The Hard Life.
The Poor Mouth.
The Third Policeman.

CLAUDE OLLIER, *The Mise-en-Scène.*

PATRIK OUŘEDNÍK, *Europeana.*

FERNANDO DEL PASO, *Palinuro of Mexico.*

ROBERT PINGET, *The Inquisitory.*
Mahu or The Material.
Trio.

RAYMOND QUENEAU, *The Last Days.*
Odile.
Pierrot Mon Ami.
Saint Glinglin.

ANN QUIN, *Berg.*
Passages.
Three.
Tripticks.

ISHMAEL REED, *The Free-Lance Pallbearers.*
The Last Days of Louisiana Red.
Reckless Eyeballing.
The Terrible Threes.
The Terrible Twos.
Yellow Back Radio Broke-Down.

JULIÁN RÍOS, *Larva: A Midsummer Night's Babel.*
Poundemonium.

AUGUSTO ROA BASTOS, *I the Supreme.*

JACQUES ROUBAUD, *The Great Fire of London.*

Hortense in Exile.
Hortense Is Abducted.
The Plurality of Worlds of Lewis.
The Princess Hoppy.
Some Thing Black.

LEON S. ROUDIEZ, *French Fiction Revisited.*

VEDRANA RUDAN, *Night.*

LYDIE SALVAYRE, *The Company of Ghosts.*
The Lecture.

LUIS RAFAEL SÁNCHEZ, *Macho Camacho's Beat.*

SEVERO SARDUY, *Cobra & Maitreya.*

NATHALIE SARRAUTE, *Do You Hear Them?*
Martereau.
The Planetarium.

ARNO SCHMIDT, *Collected Stories.*
Nobodaddy's Children.

CHRISTINE SCHUTT, *Nightwork.*

GAIL SCOTT, *My Paris.*

JUNE AKERS SEESE,
Is This What Other Women Feel Too?
What Waiting Really Means.

AURELIE SHEEHAN, *Jack Kerouac Is Pregnant.*

VIKTOR SHKLOVSKY, *Knight's Move.*
A Sentimental Journey: Memoirs 1917-1922.
Theory of Prose.
Third Factory.
Zoo, or Letters Not about Love.

JOSEF ŠKVORECKÝ,
The Engineer of Human Souls.

CLAUDE SIMON, *The Invitation.*

GILBERT SORRENTINO, *Aberration of Starlight.*
Blue Pastoral.
Crystal Vision.
Imaginative Qualities of Actual Things.
Mulligan Stew.
Pack of Lies.
The Sky Changes.
Something Said.
Splendide-Hôtel.
Steelwork.
Under the Shadow.

W. M. SPACKMAN, *The Complete Fiction.*

GERTRUDE STEIN, *Lucy Church Amiably.*
The Making of Americans.
A Novel of Thank You.

PIOTR SZEWC, *Annihilation.*

STEFAN THEMERSON, *Hobson's Island.*
Tom Harris.

JEAN-PHILIPPE TOUSSAINT, *Television.*

ESTHER TUSQUETS, *Stranded.*

DUBRAVKA UGRESIC, *Lend Me Your Character.*
Thank You for Not Reading.

MATI UNT, *Things in the Night.*

LUISA VALENZUELA, *He Who Searches.*

BORIS VIAN, *Heartsnatcher.*

PAUL WEST, *Words for a Deaf Daughter & Gala.*

CURTIS WHITE, *America's Magic Mountain.*
The Idea of Home.
Memories of My Father Watching TV.
Monstrous Possibility: An Invitation to Literary Politics.
Requiem.

DIANE WILLIAMS, *Excitability: Selected Stories.*
Romancer Erector.

DOUGLAS WOOLF, *Wall to Wall.*
Ya! & John-Juan.

PHILIP WYLIE, *Generation of Vipers.*

MARGUERITE YOUNG, *Angel in the Forest.*
Miss MacIntosh, My Darling.

REYOUNG, *Unbabbling.*

ZORAN ŽIVKOVIĆ, *Hidden Camera.*

LOUIS ZUKOFSKY, *Collected Fiction.*

SCOTT ZWIREN, *God Head.*

FOR A FULL LIST OF PUBLICATIONS, VISIT:
www.dalkeyarchive.com